Chaos in the Cathedral

Mark Bartholomew

For
Little Eliza
and in memory of Cherrie, Rene and Maureen

Acknowledgements:

Barry and Liz Bartholomew, Lucy Butcher,
Margot Allison and Philip Daws from Waterstones.
Stuart Hobday, Willow Class, Steiner School,
Thornham

First published
NOVEMBER 2006 in Great Britain by

Educational Printing Services Limited
Albion Mill, Water Street, Great Harwood, Blackburn BB6 7QR
Telephone: (01254) 882080   Fax: (01254) 882010
E-mail: enquiries@eprint.co.uk   Website: www.eprint.co.uk

ISBN 1 904904 94 7
ISBN-13 978 1-904904-94-6

Contents

The City of the Dead

Darkness and chaos,
shadow . . . despair.
Foul things assail us,
they fly through the air.

A beast then appears,
it sweeps through the land.
Spreading disease,
with its deathly hand.

Can no one stop it,
for the beast must be fed.
Is there any last hope,
. . . in the city of the dead?

Medieval Lincolnshire

N

W ← → E

S

Grimsby ○

Gainsborough ○

Saviley ●

Lincoln ○

Partney ●

Spilsby ●

Navenby ●

Wainfleet ●

Brant Broughton ●

Leverton ●

Grantham ○

Stamford ○

○	Towns
●	Green Man Carvings
– – –	Route

1: The White Boar Inn
~ When the snow is deep, the sick will weep ~

"I'm so cold!" the girl pulled her cloak tight about her as she and her two companions disembarked from the ghost-grey ship which lay anchored by the riverside. Far above her a white frost clung tightly around the mighty spire of the cathedral as a vicious snowstorm blew down angrily upon the city.

"I know," said the hunched figure that climbed the last step from the dockside and rested upon his staff to catch his icy breath. "But, we must go on. If we don't find the inn before nightfall, we'll all freeze to death!"

Pulling their hoods over their heads they moved off, as the blizzard that had engulfed the great city of Lincoln continued unabated.

Within moments they'd left the icy Witham riverfront behind them, glancing back only briefly to see the masts of the ships disappear into the snowy mists. Then, they weaved their way through the maze of narrow streets that lay at the foot of the great cathedral. An eerie silence followed them and except for a few stray boatmen, the streets they wandered were deserted; Lincoln's inhabitants had wisely shut themselves away from the storm's wrath. But the blizzard couldn't stop the three strangers from looking for the man they had come to find and as they turned each new corner they stared desperately through the swirling snow, searching for the White Boar Inn.

Hastily, they slipped down Broadgate and into Saltergate where the smell of the dried fish saltings filled their nostrils. Suddenly before them, through the falling snow and swinging wildly in the gale, was a rattling wooden sign and upon it was the snarling white beast they were hunting. "At last!" gasped one of the figures as the howling wind snatched the words and tossed them into the storm. They approached the door of the inn and pushed it open praying they would find their man inside; he was their last hope!

᠅

It had taken six long days and nights cramped up in a river barge full of fish before Nathaniel, Fern and Hickory had been pitched up on the city of Lincoln's riverfront. Six days and nights with the stench of mackerel and plaice pervading everything, six days and nights with the icy wind chilling them through to the bone and the rain and then the snow falling hard upon them.

And it had been a whole month since the Wild Man of Orford and his friends had waved their goodbyes after dropping the three of them off by the small fishing port of Wainfleet, wild and remote on the east coast of Lincolnshire. There they had wandered the countryside searching for the wherabouts of one Robin Hood. But whichever name they used to make enquiries whether it be: 'The Hooded Man', 'Robin of the Wood', 'Robert of Locksley' or 'The Green Outlaw', it seemed that no-one knew where to find him!

And yet there were so many tales to tell; stories of his deeds and of his valour and of his adventures in the forest. They had become lost in a labyrinth of what was true and what was only myth or legend. But just when they had begun to believe that no such person existed, they met an old carpenter who said he was cousin to one of Robin's band of outlaws. He told them how his relative now lived in Lincoln and went under the name of Bill Redman and that was why they now stood outside the White Boar Inn.

"It's a rotten night to be out!" The fat innkeeper eyed the three hooded newcomers suspiciously as they entered his tavern. Slowly, the tallest of the three drew back his cloak and revealed the face of an old man. Furrowed lines were etched upon his temple and a wispy white beard sprouted on his chin but his eyes were bright and lively.

"We're looking for someone." Nathaniel looked the barman in the eye.

"Who?" asked the innkeeper meeting his gaze, sternly.

The old man glanced down at the two children beside him and then turned back to the innkeeper, "His name is Bill Redman."

"Never heard of him," he replied gruffly, as he wiped clean a pewter tankard.

"He may be known to you by a different name," the old man continued.

"Well, what is it then?"

"Will Scarlet," and the innkeeper dropped the tankard with a crash!

❧

Swiftly, the three hooded travellers were shown into the back room of the tavern and the innkeeper shut the heavy wooden door hard behind him. The room was dark and smokey and the logs in the hearth crackled and spat like an old witch, whilst a heady smell of ale and mead filled the musty air.

"How do you know that name?" the innkeeper asked, with a worried look upon his face.

"It's common enough knowledge in the right places," Nathaniel Drinkstone retorted.

"We were informed that the innkeeper of the White Boar would know of his whereabouts, but if we are wasting our time here then we shall leave immediately."

"Now hold on a minute," the innkeeper's voice softened. "I have to be careful you know. After all Will Scarlet is still a wanted man." His eyes darted to the two smaller figures and then he gasped in shock as they pulled down their hoods.

"Don't worry about these two," the old man stated, as the green children smiled mischievously at the stunned innkeeper, "they won't harm you!"

But the innkeeper instinctively backed away and spluttered out, "What are they?"

"Children, of course," Nathaniel replied. "I know children frighten some people . . . small, smelly, unruly things! But these two are quite well mannered you know." Nathaniel smiled at his two young companions whilst the innkeeper looked on, bemused by his sarcasm.

"But . . . but . . . they're green!" he exclaimed.

"They're the same as you and me," Nathaniel continued, "just a different colour, that's all. Now quickly, where can we find Scarlet?"

The innkeeper regained his composure and sat down upon a three-legged stool. "You cannot tell anyone I told you anything or I will lose this tavern and probably my head." His piggy eyes blinked with worry in the half-light and despite the cold, beads of sweat dribbled down his chubby cheeks.

"Do you think we want to bring attention to ourselves?" The old man was getting angry and impatient. "Now, tell us what you know!"

The innkeeper held his head in his hands and let out a great sigh. "Well, what I tell you won't do you much good anyway because poor old Will is stuck in the cathedral quarter under strict quarantine with the rest of 'em. No-one is allowed in or out!"

"Why is it under quarantine?" The children noted the concern in Nathaniel's voice.

The innkeeper looked up at the old man and spoke in a frightened whisper, "*The Foul Death* is raging and he has been sorely stricken with it."

The two green children looked at the innkeeper and then at Nathaniel with questioning eyes. "What does all this mean?" Fern finally asked.

Nathaniel turned toward her looking downcast, "It means that the plague has come to Lincoln and worse still . . . Will Scarlet's got it!"

2: The Foul Death

~ Frogs and toads, rats and mice
- cures for plagues, are never nice ~

"**W**ell, it's clear what we have to do!" Nathaniel stated, as he sat outside the inn, gazing up the hill at the great cathedral that stood above them. "We have no choice but to get into the cathedral quarter and find Scarlet before it's too late."

"There is so much I do not understand though." Hickory's voice was quizzical, his face anxious, "What is this *Foul Death*?"

"I'm guessing that it's a disease like the ones Meg Fletcher told me about," Fern interrupted.

"That's right!" Nathaniel answered. Some diseases are not dangerous: a sneeze, a few spots here and there, a little stomach cramp, but others spread like wild ivy and kill many with one fell swoop."

"And the *Foul Death* is like that?" Hickory asked, hesitantly.

"Yes, I'm afraid so," Nathaniel replied. "Some diseases are spread through water, some through the air and many believe the *Foul Death* is transmitted through touch. But I'm not so sure."

"Are there no cures for it?" Fern looked up at him.

"Many have been tried! Different potions and ointments, medicines and balms - but nothing seems to work."

Then, the old man's voice became more jovial. "Some people have given more bizarre ideas a try. I have heard that folk hold live frogs to the boils hoping that they will suck up the poison and others use cow dung and live chickens' bottoms."

"Yuck!" the children cried in unison. "They must be really stupid!" exclaimed Hickory.

"Aye lad, perhaps they are, but if your family are dying all around then you'd try anything I suspect, so do not be too harsh upon them."

Fern's eyes looked far away as she thought of what lengths she would go to, to find her own father or bring back her mother, or even to restore her memories of her old homeland. "So, once you have it, you cannot survive?" Her face was thoughtful, yet nervous, as she met Nathaniel's gaze.

"You mean Will Scarlet's as good as dead already?" the old man had read her thoughts.

"Yes!" she replied, "I suppose I do!"

"Well, some survive," Nathaniel's voice was more upbeat, "the strong and the healthy

- but Will Scarlet is an old man now by all accounts. How long he can hold out for, I don't know."

"Yet, if we can reach him in time, perhaps I can aid him," Fern pressed her woollen pack hard against her where inside were her precious herbs.

"Yes, that's my hope also," the old man put his arm around her shoulder. "Your skills may be just what's needed here."

"But first we have to get past the guard and into the quarantined quarter itself," Hickory cut in.

Nathaniel rose to his feet, turned and pulled the children up. "That is the least of our worries lad." And he looked away up the hill at the stone giant that looked down upon them. "Once inside we may of course contract the disease ourselves and then we still have to get out again. No one will be expecting people to go voluntarily into a plague ridden city but getting out, well, that's a different story."

The children's shoulders drooped heavily and then the sky darkened, the wind howled wolfishly and the snow fell.

3: Bishop Hugh

~ A virtuous priest is hard to find ~

The body lay limply on the straw bed - lank, lifeless and still. Large lumps, as big as apples, were under the man's armpits and around the glands of his neck. All over his torso dark boils wept out a black secretion. On the windowsill a long tapered candle flickered as the shutters rattled with the storm's icy breath. A faint, almost inaudible breath, sighed from the body's lips, then it went silent . . . and the candle blew out!

❧

Outside the dying man's room, far below his resting place, two men-at-arms in the black and gold livery of the Gild of Lincoln exchanged gossip as they patrolled up and down the wooden palisade that separated the quarantined cathedral quarter from the rest of the city.

Below them, thick snow lay upon the cobbled streets muffling the footsteps of three white robed figures as they slipped under the shadow of the palisade and out of the sight of the night patrol. They had skirted the centre of the city and had approached the cathedral quarter from the northern side, slipping along Bailgate and the closed shopfronts and they now stood under the wooden picket fence.

Silently, Nathaniel, Fern and Hickory crawled along the cobbles until they reached the heaps of snow that had drifted up against the palisade wall. Then, holding their breath, they tunnelled into the mounds until they could feel the sharpened stakes of the bottom of the picket fence. A white cold surrounded them, wet snow blocked out any light but they felt their way along and pushed themselves underneath the wall. The stakes pinched them and Nathaniel struggled to arch his shoulders under the wooden fence. For a brief moment he was stuck but Fern pulled him from the front and Hickory pushed him from behind and with a snow-muffled cry, the old man was finally propelled into the quarantined quarter.

Up on the parapet one of the guards halted in his tracks and peered down below into the cathedral square. Fern and Hickory slinked into the shadows and held their breath. Nathaniel lay flat on the ground, his face buried in the snow. He dared not move and then he too held his breath, though he was sure he would be spotted.

"What's the matter?" the other guard called

over to his companion.

"Thought I heard something!"

"Probably rats . . . only thing that's alive in there, I reckon."

"I guess so, I can't see anything." The two guards stared down into the square, their gaze passing over the body of the old man without noticing him.

"Come on, I've still got some wine to drink," the first guard grumbled, and with that the guards disappeared back into the tower at the end of the palisade.

Fern and Hickory rushed out into the square and helped Nathaniel to sit up. Then they disrobed from their stolen white ermine cloaks and hid them by the wall for later use. But as Nathaniel sat there and pulled out lumps of snow from his mouth he suddenly recoiled from the sight in front of him. A limp, grey arm was sticking out from a hastily dug trench, its decaying fingers clenched in a defiant fist in the frozen air. The old man instantly realised they had entered the quarantined area right by the plague pit and quickly he pulled the children away from the mass grave.

In horror, all three of them ran silently through the snow-covered streets and entered the Minster Yard in the middle of the quarantined quarter. Under the rising spires of the great cathedral they stopped to catch their breath as a host of gargoyles, angels and saints stared down upon them from all sides.

"Well, we're inside," stated Hickory. "Now what do we do?"

"We have two choices, I think," Nathaniel looked around at the buildings within the cathedral close.

"What are they?" Hickory responded.

"Go to the local inn or seek out the man in charge."

"Who would that be?" the boy replied.

"The Bishop, of course," Nathaniel smiled.

The children winced. Their only knowledge of Bishops had been their encounter with Guy de Bellambe, the Abbot of Bury St. Edmunds and it had not been a pleasant meeting. The two children looked at each other then replied in unison, "The inn!"

Nathaniel laughed, "So be it," and they set off through the grey and dreary streets looking for an inn.

*

As they silently roamed the deserted city they couldn't help but notice the numerous red crosses that were daubed upon the doors of the houses and shops they passed. "It means the plague has visited," Nathaniel met the children's enquiring gaze. There were so many that they stood out like open sores against the snowy white streets, echoing the ravages of the disease that raged inside.

When at last they found a tavern it too had the now familiar fearsome sign upon its great oak door. In fact the Black Bull was completely boarded up and little sign of any life existed inside at all. As they stood outside in the snow they thought they heard the anguished cry of a woman rise out of the emptiness of the inn, but they couldn't be sure it wasn't just the whining of the wind, so they left the tavern to its despair.

Once again, they stood in the square and found they were left with the only remaining option. "I know you have reservations children," Nathaniel looked down upon his companions with understanding, "but not all churchmen are like Guy de Bellambe. The Bishop of Lincoln is one Hugh of Avalon, a fair and well-respected man, I've heard."

"Then we have no choice but to see him," Hickory's face looked worried.

"I agree," Nathaniel rested his hand on Hickory's shoulder, "but we must be on our guard for the Bishop represents power and authority and Will Scarlet is an outlaw after all. The Bishop might not harm us but he might well be after Scarlet."

"That is of course if this Bishop Hugh is still alive!" Fern spoke gravely, as she looked toward the ghostly grey outline of the Bishop's Palace.

But Bishop Hugh was indeed alive and trying desperately to save his flock. "Another case at the Black Bull, your worship," the attendant priest looked terrified as he approached the rotund cleric.

"Who has it?" Hugh turned to meet the priest's eyes.

"Eleanor Rathbone, I'm afraid."

Hugh stood up and moved from behind his desk to gaze out of the window and down Steep Hill to the tavern. "Poor little mite," the Bishop replied and in the candlelight a tear formed in his eyes and he turned away from the attendant and wiped the cuff of his surplice across his face. This was no time to show emotion, he thought to himself. I must be strong; John and Katherine Rathbone need my shoulder to lean on now.

Suddenly, the attendant's ears pricked up, "What was that?" he cried.

"Sounded like a knock on the front door,

Edmund," the Bishop replied, calmly.

"But who could it be at this hour?" the priest almost ran to the stairs.

"Visitors, I expect," the Bishop sat back down near the fire, and waited. Moments later he heard raised voices below.

"It's far too late!" the priest was trying to send someone packing. Bishop Hugh moved to the top of the stairs, intrigued to find out who was calling at such an hour.

"Let them in," he called down to the front door.

As the visitors climbed the staircase the Bishop walked back into his chamber and stood by the fire. The priest then ushered in three strangers dressed in hooded cloaks. "I'm sorry, your worship."

"It's alright, Edmund," the Bishop smiled warmly at his attendant and then he turned to his visitors. "Now, how can I help you?"

Nathaniel and the children drew down their hoods as the attendant gasped in wonder. "Your worship!" the priest exclaimed, as he stood between the children and the Bishop, "run for your life!" But the Bishop just laughed and patted the priest's shoulder indulgently. "I don't think we have anything to fear, Edmund, in fact I would say they look a lot more frightened of me."

"We have met a god-man before," said Hickory. "I didn't like him!"

"I see," said the Bishop. "Perhaps, I am not like him?"

"I hope not!" Nathaniel interrupted. "The boy is talking about Abbot Guy of Bury St. Edmunds."

"Oh, then I understand his feelings. But not all of us are like the Abbot."

"I'm glad to hear it," Hickory replied, though he watched the Bishop with apprehension.

"Edmund, would you be so kind as to fetch our visitors a bowl of warm pottage, I'm sure they are hungry."

"Yes, your worship, if you are sure," and the attendant scampered off toward the kitchens.

"Come and warm yourselves and tell me everything, I imagine you have quite a tale to tell."

"You are right, there," Nathaniel answered, as he slumped wearily down onto the chair by the fireside. The children fell to the floor by his feet and through tired eyes they watched the red flames in the hearth dance around the great log.

The old man waited until the attendant had brought in their pottage and as he closed the door behind him, told the Bishop of their quest and how they had come to be in Lincoln.

"So, what do you want of me?" Hugh rose from his chair and stoked the fire.

"We are looking for someone," Nathaniel answered, unsure as to how the Bishop would react to their search for an outlaw.

"Who is it you seek?"

"He goes by the name of Bill Redman," Nathaniel whispered the name. "Have you heard of him?"

"Yes," Hugh of Avalon smiled, "I know Bill Redman alright, although I tend to call him Will," and he winked at the children, who grinned tentatively in reply.

"I also know where to find him," the Bishop continued, but then his face slipped into seriousness and his eyes fell to the floor. "But his life hangs in the balance, I'm afraid. I attended him last night and gave him the last rites. He is old and won't last long now. I have never seen anyone nearer to their maker."

"Then we must go to him at once!" Fern's voice burst into urgency as she drew herself away from the mesmerising flames.

"Steady, my child," Hugh retorted, "there is nothing that can be done."

"No," Nathaniel rose from his chair, "the girl is right your worship. She may be able to save him, she has . . ." the old man stumbled on the right words to describe Fern's powers, "she has a gift for healing."

"This I must see," and the Bishop grabbed his cloak, opened the door and they all left to find the dying outlaw.

4: Will Scarlet

~ Red is the colour of life ~

"This is called 'Askantha'," Fern spoke softly as she stood over the limp body of Will Scarlet and pressed the dried herbs upon his fevered brow.

Bishop Hugh studied the herbs with interest, "God's medicine," he murmured.

"Nature's healing," Fern replied.

"Perhaps a little of both then, my child," the Bishop wasn't convinced that Will would see daybreak.

"He's so hot. His body is on fire!" Hickory felt the outlaw's hand.

"Do you not have diseases like this?" The Bishop looked quizzically at the boy.

"No, at least nothing I can remember."

"We have our herbs and plants and they seem to keep us from harm," Fern interrupted, as she bent over to pour some of her herbal potion down the dying man's throat.

Scarlet gulped at the liquid and then lay his head back on his straw pillow and slipped back into a restless sleep. They all watched him closely as his eyes blinked repeatedly and beads of sweat trickled down his forehead.

23

And then a calmness seemed to come upon him. His wrinkled old hands stopped twitching by his side. His whole body ceased trembling and suddenly he grew quite still.

"It's almost over," Hugh whispered sadly.

"No, I do not think so," replied Nathaniel. "Look at his face!"

The Bishop studied the dying outlaw carefully; the beads of sweat had dried up and the fever seemed to have passed, but his eyes were closed and the Bishop moved towards him.

"Wait!" Fern held Hugh's arm and he halted. "Watch," she murmured under her breath.

On the bed, Scarlet lay motionless, as if he had been carved from stone, but upon his face a change could be seen. The soft grey mask of death that had lain upon him for so many days was slipping away and some colour was returning to his cheeks.

"He still has some strength inside him," Fern spoke softly. "He's been pulled back from the edge of death . . . he may yet recover."

The Bishop remained cautious, but he couldn't deny what he saw before him. "You have great skills in healing young lady," he stared at Fern as the spark of an idea came to life. So far it had been a dreadful year for the Bishop, but perhaps now, at long last, some hope was returning.

5: The Gildmaster

~ For silver and gold, men's souls are sold ~

"How many potions today?" the tall, well dressed man spoke quietly to the militia guard by the palisade wall.

"There have been no requests, Gildmaster," he replied.

"None!?" the man barked angrily.

"None," the guard repeated, timidly. He knew the power the Gildmaster wielded in Lincoln and he didn't like making him cross.

Only last week, when the Gildmaster had turned up by the palisade in the dead of night, the guard had thought it odd that a man as wealthy as Giles Blackforth should come near this plague-infested rathole. But he'd soon learnt that the Gildmaster had trade in mind and he didn't trust anyone with his business other than himself. Even so, it was a risky venture. No one was supposed to enter or leave the quarantined quarter and the fear of contamination had seduced everyone on either side of the hastily erected wall. Still, business was business and if the right price was involved goods could pass through anywhere and Giles Blackforth always had the right price.

"It seems as if the rumours are true, sire," the guard was inwardly pleased that he could give the Gildmaster some bad news. He hated the way Blackforth had profited from the poor souls dying inside the quarter. As Gildmaster he was supposed to help the families of the dying, not set up a quarantine and bleed them dry.

"What rumours?" Blackforth was annoyed, he thought he knew everything that happened in this city.

"About these mysterious green children that turned up a couple of days ago," the guard continued.

"What of them?" Blackforth feigned knowledge. He didn't want some lowly guard thinking he wasn't up with the latest gossip.

"Seems like they're curing all the poor beggars. Some green magic they reckon - something to do with herbs!"

"Really," Blackforth's fingers twitched, nervously. "Where did these green children come from?"

"Just appeared from nowhere with some old fellow, so they say. Tossed out from the storm or blown down from heaven to save them all, who knows? Still, bit of a problem for you isn't it Gildmaster?"

"No problem at all," Blackforth kept his

cool, though inwardly he was seething. "I have plenty of other outlets to keep me busy."

"What are you going to do with that lot, then?" The guard seemed to be laughing at the Gildmaster.

Blackforth looked down at the vials of grimy black liquid that sat in the crate on the ground before his feet. 'Blackforth's Plague remedy' he had named the vile potion inside them; a mixture of ditchwater and honey with about as much medicinal use as a dead dog. Still, they'd become a lucrative little sideline and the Gildmaster did not like losing trade, especially when it was with a captive audience ready to part with plenty of cash for even the flimsiest hint of a cure to the *Foul Death*.

Blackforth's Plague Remedy

Marvellous, miraculous cures for

'The Foul Death', 'The Devil's Itch' and 'Puddle Fever'

Price: Only One Silver Penny

Finally, Blackforth's temper got the better of him, he kicked the crate angrily, two of the bottles smashed and he swore out loudly.

"Looks like you're out of business, Gildmaster," the guard risked a smile at Blackforth's misfortune.

"We'll see about that," he snapped and leaving his crate in the street he strode off, angrily, to his townhouse.

6: The Stone Giant
~ *It's not always the cream that rises to the top* ~

The Bishop was a round figure with a warm, open face, but crinkled lines were etched around his eyes and he walked along the streets of Lincoln as if he carried a great burden upon his shoulders.

"How did the plague come to this city?" Nathaniel turned to him as they strode toward Will Scarlet's lodgings, underneath the shadow of a brooding, grumpy-looking cluster of clouds.

The priest suddenly looked downcast. "It has not been a good year, Nathaniel. Last October a terrible earthquake shook the cathedral to its very foundations. Beautiful statues, gruesome gargoyles, arches and windows all smashed to pieces. The roof was damaged and, at one point, I thought the whole place was going to cave in upon our heads. Then, my pride got the better of me."

"How so?"

"I knew the plague was about but still I sent out for workmen, builders and craftsmen to come and rebuild our beautiful cathedral," the Bishop paused for a moment, "and many flocked to our assistance. Problem was, somebody brought the plague with them. I blame myself."

"It's not your fault," Nathaniel spoke warmly. He knew the Bishop was a good man.

"Thank you, Nathaniel, but it is difficult not to accept some of the blame, especially when I see so many of my people dying around me and I realise that I don't possess the skills to save them. There comes a time when praying is not enough and I must admit that in the darkest of days even my faith in the Lord himself has been shaken."

At the foot of Scarlet's lodgings they stopped and Nathaniel put a hand upon the Bishop's shoulder as they looked up to see a crisp, clear green light shining from the dying outlaw's window. "Perhaps your luck is changing." Nathaniel spoke softly and then they entered.

෴

Up in the chamber of his townhouse, outside the cathedral quarter, Giles Blackforth sat down next to a raging fire and poured himself a tankard of warm wine. Freshly delivered from the far-flung lands of Burgundy, this was a rare treat, which the Master of the Gilds of Lincoln knew he justly deserved. But as he handled the bottle it had come in and tried to decipher the Burgundian script upon it, his mind could not evade the thought of his own bottles left idle in the street by the palisade walls. Damn them! The bitter taste of losing trade soured the wine he supped and he stared into the flames and thought of what to do next. He had plenty of power to act with, that was for sure; the Gilds of Lincoln were amongst the oldest and most influential societies in all of England and as such the Gildmaster was a powerful man.

The irony was that Blackforth was actually from the rough streets of the riverfront, born out of wedlock to a drunken serving girl. At twelve years of age he had managed to secure himself a smith's apprenticeship in Silver Street and slowly but surely he worked his way into his master's affections. Once he had worked his seven years he became a journeyman and then he wormed his way into the affections of his master's daughter. By the age of twenty-five he took over the silver shop of Simon Brindle for himself and soon became a master silversmith.

Now he had become upright, rich and as powerful as his hopes could ever have imagined, but he still didn't quite know how to stop wringing money out of people. The devious intrigues, plots and political machinations he had made to get to his lofty perch had been as intricate as any of his silverwork and now, with perhaps the exception of the Bishop, he saw himself as the most important man in the city, especially with Hugh of Avalon stuck inside his beloved cathedral. And so he was damned sure that two odd green children were not going to get the better of him!

"It's still too early to tell for sure but he seems to be getting better," Nathaniel smiled as he told Fern and Hickory the latest news on Will Scarlet. "It may be that in a few days he'll be well enough to talk."

"About Robin Hood?" Hickory was excited.

"Hopefully," replied Nathaniel.

"Well, he may be getting better but many others in the quarter are still falling prey to this dreadful disease." The Bishop was looking at Fern. "It is stalking the city, waiting on corners, striking anyone, at anytime - like a snake."

"I know," she drew her eyes up to meet his. "And you need my help again?"

There was a flicker of hope in the Bishop's eyes. "Yes, desperately. I see clearly now how you have helped old Will."

So, over the next few days Bishop Hugh led Fern with her precious healing herbs through the streets. Together they administered their medicine to the sick of the city. And something clear and fresh, something green and natural fell upon Lincoln. It was as if the city was full of flowers and meadows and yet the snow continued to fall and the pale, weak, winter sun sat low and melancholy in the sky above.

7: Waking Days

~ *Sorrow and Joy live hand in hand when foul
disease stalks the land* ~

"She's only three years old!" the cry was a
tormented one, a gasping, breathless
howl of despair aimed at everyone and
no one.

John Rathbone stared helplessly at his wife
as she cried out and then he turned back to
the tiny body that lay upon the bed. The face
was as white as the snow that lay all around
the streets outside, the girl's hair was lank
and lifeless and dark rings were etched
around her closed eyes. Rathbone knew that
he would have to bury his daughter the
following morning; his pearl, his most
precious possession. He had only just laid to
rest his mother. So he gripped hard upon the
end of the bed and stood firm and resolute
and then he took his wife in his arms as she
buried her face in his chest.

Moments later a gentle rapping fell upon
the tavern door and both John and Katherine
Rathbone looked up from their desolation.

"I'll go." John Rathbone stroked the tears
away from his wife's face and walked slowly
to the door.

"Good evening, John." It was Bishop Hugh.

"Evening, your worship."

"I'm so sorry to hear about Eleanor."

"Thank you, Hugh," Rathbone replied in a lifeless monotone.

The two men stood on the doorstep whilst the slight frame of Fern appeared from behind the round figure of the Bishop. She moved quickly and made to enter the tavern.

Rathbone took a step backward as she crossed into the light of the hallway and from behind him his wife gave out a gasp of surprise.

"This young lady believes she can help you," Hugh spoke quietly, ignoring the desolate couple's reaction to the green girl.

Fern moved straight to the tiny bed where she found the girl wrapped up in a blanket. She pulled back the coverlet to expose her face and looked long and hard into the girl's eyes and then she listened carefully to her chest. All at once she pulled out a handful of herbs from her bag and studied them in silence as the Bishop and the Rathbones watched on. Then she picked out two particular leaves and her eyes darted to the fireplace and the cooking pot that sat upon it.

"Mrs Rathbone," Fern turned to meet the mother's eyes. "Could you bring me some boiling water, please?"

"Yes! Yes of course," Katherine Rathbone moved as if in a trance, a waking nightmare that now had brought a green girl to stand over her dead child!

But her husband was not so entranced by Fern's presence, "I'll have no witchcraft here!" John Rathbone stood up sharply and put a firm hand upon his wife's arm to prevent her fetching the water.

"Do you think I would have anything to do with witchcraft, John?" Bishop Hugh spoke calmly but firmly.

"This girl believes she can help Ellie. I have seen with my own eyes what good she has done all over the quarter. Where our medicines have failed she has brought healing, when our prayers have failed she has brought hope."

"But she's already dead!" John Rathbone's voice was barely a whisper as he let go of his wife's arm and sat back upon his stool.

"I know, John. But let her try. She believes she can still do something." Hugh put a hand on the innkeeper's shoulder.

"Please John. What have we got to lose?" Katherine Rathbone fell to the floor at her husband's feet and held his hands in her own. Her husband bowed his head deep in thought and the inn fell silent.

"Alright," he finally answered. "Do what you can, if there is anything to be done other than to bury her."

Immediately, Katherine rose and brought a pot of boiling water to Fern. In turn, she rubbed the leaves that she held and dropped them into the pot. Instantly, a green steam rose upward filling the inn with a sweet aroma. Fern took some up with a wooden spoon and blew upon the remedy to cool it. Then, whilst her mother lifted Ellie's head, Fern tipped a little of the potion into her mouth. Hardly any of the brew managed to slip past her lips however and most of the green liquid tumbled down her chin and dripped onto her best dress - her burial dress.

Fern tried again with another spoonful and this time more of the mixture slipped passed her blue lips and down her throat. She repeated this a number of times and when she was satisfied she let Katherine rest her daughter's head back upon the pillow.

"Now what?" asked John.

"We wait," replied Fern.

And wait they did. It was nearly an hour before anyone in the inn spoke or even stirred from their stools.

But then, just as Katherine Rathbone had

slipped into a fitful and uneasy sleep with her head nestled upon her husband's shoulder, she awoke with a start. "She's alive!" Her voice was excited and anxious too. It was as if she had awoken from a nightmare.

"Steady, love." John Rathbone stroked her hair but Katherine stood up knowingly.

"Listen," she said calmly, "just listen."

They bent their heads even closer to the tiny figure upon the bed straining their thoughts, their inner selves, toward the child and they listened. At first, Bishop Hugh could hear nothing, except the beat of his own heart, but then as he closed his eyes he heard the sound they had all longed for. A soft, rasping breathing sound. The sound of a child not dead and silent, but sleeping, alive and sleeping.

Katherine burst across the room, her husband close behind and they hugged the girl tightly. Young Eleanor blinked her eyes, then rubbed them and tried to pull herself up, but it was too much for her yet. She lent back against her pillow, her face still pale - deathly pale - but her blue eyes now danced around the room as she wondered what all the fuss was about.

It made Fern feel good to see these people

smile again, to rejoice in something so precious given back to them. She remembered fondly how the Fletcher twins reacted when she'd brought Nunty, their grandmother, out of her sickness, though the Fletchers and Woolpit now seemed far, far away.

"Well, we must be off," Bishop Hugh rose from his seat and Fern stood up behind him.

"How can we ever thank you?" John Rathbone crossed back to them and embraced Fern and then the Bishop.

"Keep faith, John. Just keep faith," Hugh replied, as he put a firm arm on the innkeeper's shoulder.

⚜

As they stepped back out into the empty streets, the Bishop took Fern's hand in his and turned to face her. "What you have done in there is a miracle. In fact, I have only ever heard of one person that could do such a thing."

"Where?" asked Fern innocently.

Hugh grinned, " In the bible . . . his name was Jesus."

"Oh, I've heard of him," Fern smiled.

"I'm glad to hear of it," Hugh replied.

"Was he a great healer?"

Hugh stopped and stood silently for a

moment and then he put his hand upon Fern's shoulder and he too smiled. "Yes my child, he was a great healer . . . of body and soul." Hugh's faith itself had been shaken these last few weeks, but somehow the arrival of the children had re-awoken his beliefs - for were they not creatures of the Lord, sent to aid them in their hour of need? Though many would be outraged at their lack of Christianity, no doubt call them heretic and try to burn them, Hugh saw only good in their arrival at such a calamitous time.

The sun shone, weakly, through the stained glass window of the north transept, but even with such a sad, pale light, bright colours danced on the stone floor of the cathedral. Fern stood transfixed, watching the red, gold and green shapes playing tag before her feet. Then a great cloud shut out the light and the dancing colours disappeared. Thunder rumbled somewhere high above and the sky turned black.

Fern was tired. More tired than she had ever been. Worn down by endless hours attending the sick, she was suddenly overcome with the enormity of the disaster that surrounded her and threatened to swallow her up whole like some great beast. It was true; she had cured many of the sick. But, each new day others fell foul of the disease and her dwindling supply of herbs would not last much longer, she knew that. And then what would happen? How long could she keep the disease at bay? Would they all succumb to it? And then there was their own quest. Would they ever find Robin Hood? Was he their father? Why wasn't he searching for them? And most of all, when would she see her beloved trees again?

༈

Suddenly, it was all too much for her and she sat down, heavily, upon a pew and started to cry. Tears fell upon the stones and she buried her head in her hands, ashamed at her lack of resolve.

"Why are you crying girl?" Nathaniel's heart had missed a beat when he had seen Fern weeping in the corner of the cathedral. As soon as he had come across her limp body huddled upon the pew he feared the worst and as she turned her tearful eyes up toward him, he thought her pale face and limp state could only mean one thing.

But Fern smiled weakly as he bent down toward her. "Don't be afraid, Nathaniel. I don't have the *Foul Death*. I weep only because I miss the woods. There is a longing inside of me which I cannot truly explain. Too long have I been under the shadow of these stone buildings." Her face looked out through the great stained glass window of the nave and far, far beyond to the tiny copse of trees way below the city and out of reach.

"Look Nathaniel," she pointed out to the clouds and a sliver of sunshine reappeared like a strand of golden hair. "Spring is coming," she smiled, and then a memory came back to her out of the darkness. "Soon, it will be my waking day." Nathaniel looked perplexed. "It's the day I entered the world," she said, in answer to the old man's questioning stare.

"Your birthday you mean."

"Yes, that's it." Her mind wandered, "Hickory's is a day after mine. In fact, all our people are born in the springtime."

Just like the animals, thought Nathaniel.

"This will be my fourteenth spring," Fern grinned as her memory came back to life.

"And how old will Hickory be?" Nathaniel sat down on the pew next to her.

"He will be twelve." But as the last words slipped from her lips the clouds blocked out the strand of sunshine and Fern's head dropped again. "How much longer!" her voice was weak and full of sorrow and Nathaniel had no words to give her, but then she turned back to him and she spoke more calmly, "Yet I will endure," her fingers gripped hard upon the wood of the pew, "and this feeling will pass," she said, resolutely.

Nathaniel put a fatherly arm around her shoulder. "I understand," he whispered softly. He stood up and turned away from her sadness. There was nothing he could do or say. He knew that Fern would rise above this current darkness, he knew the strength within her, but he also understood the emptiness that lay there too. He also had wandered far from his home and his people many years ago and he knew that nobody could help in such times of homesickness.

Sure enough, an hour or so later, Fern was back tending to the sick again, with a merry voice and a light skip in her step. Yet Nathaniel looked carefully at her and her brother and he stroked his chin as he wondered just how much longer his young, green friends could continue on in this unfamiliar world.

8: Lincoln Green

*~ In the right shade of green
you can never be seen ~*

"They say he came here you know!" The old gentleman with the black ringlets of hair spoke warmly to Hickory, "Your Robin Hood." The boy's ears pricked up like a cat's. "Collected his clothes from here apparently. All dressed in Lincoln Green."

"What is that?" asked Hickory.

"A type of cloth of course. I have some here in my bag," the old gentleman showed Hickory a segment of material.

"Very special it is. The old outlaw wanted it made in just such a shade so he could hide away unseen in the forests."

Hickory took the cloth and studied it carefully. He couldn't help but notice the similarity between his own tunic and the shade of the material in his hand and a sudden hope rose within him.

"You dye the cloth blue with woad and then yellow with onion skins and you end up with Lincoln Green," continued the old man.

"What else do you know of him?" Hickory looked up into his deep brown eyes.

"I know this," and suddenly the old

gentleman sang in a deep voice.

"I'm here in the darkness, can't you see?
Look high, look low, behind each tree!
I'm here in the darkness, but you can't see
and you will never find me!"

"What's that?" Hickory asked.

"A piece of an old song. It's from 'The Ballad of Robin Hood'. Some say he wrote it himself!"

"But what does it mean? It doesn't sound very promising for us. After all, we are trying to find him!"

"All I know is that those that have gone looking for him have never returned. Once you're in his domain they say you don't see anything - there's a scatter of footsteps, arrows fly and before you know it, your men are dead and you lie at his mercy! That's why he's never been caught!"

"So why is he called Robin Hood?" The old gentleman's tales intrigued Hickory.

"I've heard it was from the time he attended an archery competition up in Yorkshire. He won the contest and was then challenged to pull his hood over his head and try to hit the target blindfold, as it were. He took up the challenge and shot perfectly, hitting the bullseye with no problem. After that he was known as Robin-in-the-hood."

Hickory looked up at the old fellow in awe. "So, who is he?"

"Well, some say he is of noble birth - a Saxon lord who had his land taken away and was forced to flee. I know that Robert of Locksley, a local landowner, went missing many years ago. I have also heard some tell that he was a crusader who wanted to hide away because of the horrors he saw in the Holy Land. He took to the woods and stayed there with his band of followers."

The old gentleman then bent down to Hickory and spoke in a near whisper. "There are some who believe that he is a spirit of the woods and forests who helps the poor and lowly. A willow-the-wisp that causes mischief and mayhem upon those who enter his hidden realm."

"What do you believe?" the boy tugged at the man's fine, purple robes.

"Oh," he stopped in his tracks. "What do I believe, eh? I believe all of them and none of them."

"What do you mean?"

"I think that Robin Hood is either a mixture of all the tales: an outlaw, a landless lord and even a woodland spirit and yet part of me also thinks he doesn't exist at all!"

The old gentleman continued walking whilst Hickory pursued him along the street, round the Minster Yard and down Steep Hill. "But," the boy hesitated for a moment, "do you think he's green, like me?"

"That, I don't know. I have never seen him, few have, except your friend up there," and he pointed at Will Scarlet's window. "Best hope he recovers."

Hickory stared up at the chamber window where the old outlaw lay gravely ill.

"Now, I must get on," and the old gentleman opened his fine front door, gave Hickory a wink and disappeared into his moneylending shop as the sign of the three golden balls rattled above, excitedly, on its master's return.

❦

"I met a strange old man today," Hickory was sitting in the Bishop's chamber with Hugh and Nathaniel.

"I thought we were the only strange old men around here," smiled Nathaniel.

"Well, he was even odder than you two," Hickory grinned. "He was dressed in a purple robe and he had a head full of black curly ringlets and a long black beard."

"Oh, that's old Aaron," answered Bishop Hugh. "Aaron is a Jew. He's a weaver of old tales and wonderful stories and he's also a very clever businessman. Unfortunately, that makes him unpopular with his rivals, which is a shame because he is a delightful man."

"I didn't know there were any Jews in Lincoln," Nathaniel said.

"Aaron came here from York when the townsfolk turned upon all the Jews there."

"Why did they do that?" Hickory asked. "Did he do something wrong?"

"The only thing old Aaron did was to be born into a different religion," Bishop Hugh answered.

"What do you mean?" Hickory did not understand what the Bishop referred to.

"Aaron believes in other stories about God than us Christians. The Muslims believe in different tales too. Sometimes it leads to arguments and ultimately, wars."

"And yet we all believe in God," Nathaniel spoke in an exasperated tone.

"That's right. But when they recruited for the last crusade and marched through York the people turned upon anyone of a different religion even though the crusade was against the Muslims. Aaron was lucky to escape with his life; many of his people were murdered in the streets, I'm afraid," the Bishop went silent.

"You see, whenever danger comes the weak and the foolhardy bully those that are different in some way," Nathaniel looked the boy in the eye. "You should know that Hickory."

"I do," and he realised that Aaron knew it too.

9: The Leech Doctor

~ The bite of a leech will make you screech ~

"He's useless!" Brother Edmund was cross. He was often cross. "He's a leechcrafter and a bloodletter. His medical knowledge is about as good as my sword-fighting skills. Opening a vein to let the evil out, drilling holes in poor soul's heads to let the devil free - utter nonsense! The poor wretches he treats are far worse after their so-called 'medicine' than they ever were before it!" Brother Edmund was telling Nathaniel about Nicholas Pevet, Lincoln's one and only doctor, who was due to arrive for an appointment with the Bishop that morning.

"What's a leechcrafter?" Hickory tugged at Nathaniel's arm.

"A good question," Nathaniel thought for a moment. "Well, a leechcrafter is someone that uses leeches to help cure the sick."

"Sounds disgusting!" cried Hickory.

"It's actually more useful than it sounds. You see the leech helps to draw blood to the wound and clean away any infection."

"Agreed, but not at the price Pevet charges and not for every single medical complaint," Brother Edmund interrupted. "I mean, how many leeches has the man got? Does he have his own leech farm? Tell him you have a chest problem and he prescribes a leech, inform him of your sore toe and he puts a leech on it. Everything from a broken leg to a common cold is dealt with by his leeches. No wonder he looks like one!"

"Now Edmund, let's keep calm shall we," Bishop Hugh intervened, but there was no stopping the little priest.

"He tried to escape, you know. Our good doctor, " Edmund continued his ranting, "once he heard there was going be a quarantine. Blackforth wouldn't let him out though. Said he was more use inside helping us, although really he just wanted him to sell his worthless potions."

"I imagine he's been very busy," said Nathaniel.

"He may be a man in demand but what real use has he been?"

"Bishop Hugh tells me that you have some healing skills and a wonderful knowledge of herbs and remedies yourself Edmund," Fern's gentle voice took the venom out of the cleric's outburst and he turned and smiled at her.

"Yes, . . . er quite," he stuttered. "Why thank you, I do dabble in the curative powers of the plants it's true, particularly teas and tisanes."

"I see," said Fern, with genuine interest. "Tell me about some of your teas, then."

"I can do even better than that," and he scurried over to the far side of the chamber where he kept a pile of manuscripts, pulled one free and handed it to Fern.

She glanced down at the priest's spidery scrawl, but to her it was a just a jumble of lines and shapes. Nathaniel had read tales to them both when they had been at Wyken Manor and he had pointed out inn signs and street names on maps that they had studied, but there had been no time to teach either Fern or Hickory to read or write. If they ever had any knowledge of a written language from their own homeland, it was lost to them now.

"I'll read them to you, shall I?" Brother Edmund said, realising that his writing meant nothing to the girl; most children were unable to read so it did not come as a surprise to the priest.

Brother Edmund's Herbal Teas

Lavender tea - A good all round tonic
Apple tea - Useful for combating fevers
Mint tea - Good for stomach aches
Rosemary tea - Refreshing for the body
Nettle tea - Revives aching bones
Thyme tea - Helpful for chest complaints
Sage tea - Cures hot flushes
Feverfew tea - Stops headaches
Camomile tea Good for insomnia

"They sound very helpful," Fern stated knowledgeably, as Brother Edmund rattled off his list of herbal infusions.

"More useful than Pevet's antiquated remedies and dubious concoctions, that's for sure!" Brother Edmund was off again, ranting and raving about the ineffectual 'quack' doctor as he called him, but then the man himself appeared at the door and the little cleric disappeared into the back rooms mumbling away.

"Ah, good doctor," the Bishop welcomed a tall, spindly figure into the chamber. "I see you are dressed to deal with our current predicament." The doctor had a large grey hat perched upon his head that flopped over his eyes like a dead cat. Over his shoulders he wore a swirling black cloak from which poked two spindly hands, one of which carried a long, thin stick to ward away plague sufferers and upon his nose was a pointed wooden beak.

"He looks less like a leech and more like a chicken," whispered Hickory.

"My appearance may look odd but it protects me from the *Foul Death*. This beak is full of rose petals and the pleasant aroma stops the disease being carried through the air toward me. And this hat ensures that the disease cannot enter through my scalp," the doctor stated, pompously.

"Do you stick frogs on people?" Hickory asked out of the blue, he was thinking of Nathaniel's tales of strange cures for the plague.

Pevet laughed, "Don't be ridiculous, child. It's toads of course!" he replied, with a haughty sniff and then looked strangely upon the green boy. "Most interesting. A lack of iron I imagine," as he pondered Hickory's skin colour.

"I have heard the rumours that these children, in fact, this odd child in particular," he said, pointing at Fern, "have been dabbling in my business. Of course amateur help is useful and I hear you have had some minor success."

"Bringing people back from the dead is more than some minor success I'd say," Bishop Hugh retorted.

"Quite, quite, well I will see Miss Rathbone tonight to make sure she is fine. But all this white witchcraft and tree magic, it's not right. I hear you're not even charging. Hardly good for the profession!"

"She's bringing hope and relief where there has been none and for as long as I can persuade her, Fern will continue to administer to the sick of this city." Hugh's voice was tired, but he spoke with a calm authority.

"Right, well if that's how it is I shall leave. But mark my words, your worship, no good will come of this herbal meddling. It may even do your eminence's solid reputation some harm."

"Thank you for your concern doctor, but I will be fine. Now, would you like something to eat before you go?" asked the Bishop.

"A few seeds perhaps," giggled Hickory. Nathaniel tried not to smile whilst the doctor ignored the strangers and strutted toward the door like a preening cockerel.

"No thank you, I must get to the Rathbones'," he said, as he checked his beak.

"Be careful! It's a low doorway at the inn. Don't forget to 'duck' down," chuckled Fern.

"Make sure Little Ellie doesn't get too 'egg-cited'," grinned Nathaniel.

"I am sure I won't excite her," said the doctor.

"I'm pretty sure of that too!" said Hickory.

"She'll be fine, he's just 'chicken' up on her," Bishop Hugh couldn't help himself and with that the doctor left, bemused, and hurried out into the night air.

As the door closed behind him the Bishop's Palace erupted in laughter, even Brother Edmund emerging from the back chambers, had a smile upon his face. And the laughter was a bright and merry sound, a spring-like sound and, for a while at least, it filled the quarantined quarter with hope.

10: The Lincoln Imp

~ For every angel there are many devils ~

While Fern helped restore the health of the people of Lincoln, Nathaniel helped rebuild their cathedral. He'd continued carving his trail of green men in some of the churches they'd passed on the way, such as Partney, Spilsby, Leverton and Navenby, and now he'd added a number of them to the great cathedral itself.

With time on his hands, Hickory too had been keen to learn the mason's craft he saw Nathaniel produce. All day long he had been labouring hard, creating a carving on the end of a long wooden pew. He chipped and chiselled, he planed and polished and eventually, to his utter joy and delight, the carven image of the Wild Man of Orford slowly emerged from the oak. The green boy's fingers carefully shaped the long strands of hair on his head, the strong wave-breaking arms and the wild sea-swimming eyes. He'd learnt quickly and Nathaniel had been a good teacher. Finally, as the winter sunlight slipped from the great cathedral's windows and the shadows grew long, Hickory rose from the pew, stood back and admired his work.

"Wonderful!" he whispered under his breath.

"Wonderful!" a tiny voice echoed above him; a thin whine, which seemed to draw scorn upon the young sculptor's work.

It was not the first time today that Hickory had felt another's presence nearby. Though he'd worked alone all day the green boy had felt as if someone or something had been watching him. Now he was certain, for the voice came from somewhere but as he looked around him, he saw no-one!

His eyes darted around the cathedral but there was nothing. He stared down the nave and could just perceive the hunched figure of Nathaniel high up on a ladder, working on the roof boss of a Wyvern. Too far away to be playing tricks though, thought Hickory. So who or what was spying on him?

Then, quite instinctively, he looked up - high up above his head. His eyes fell upon a tiny stone figure sitting cross-legged between two arches on the north side of the choir. The statue was about twelve inches tall, it had pointed ears, two tiny horns and cloven feet and it seemed to be grinning at Hickory. He was utterly transfixed by it and when Bishop Hugh wandered silently over from the Lady's Chapel, Hickory hadn't noticed that the cleric was standing next to him.

"Whatever is the matter lad?" the Bishop enquired curiously. "You look as if you've seen a ghost!"

"No, Sir!" Hickory stuttered and just looked upwards in a stupor.

Bishop Hugh's gaze followed the boy's and then he realised what he was staring at. "Oh, you've found him, have you?"

"Who is he?" Hickory replied eagerly.

"He's the Lincoln Imp," Hugh replied. "A very famous creature you know!"

"There is something strange about him," Hickory spoke as much to himself as to the Bishop.

"Well, there is an extraordinary legend about him, that's why," Hugh answered. "One day, the devil sent his imps out to play and the wind blew two of them to Lincoln. At first they were so awestruck by the great cathedral that they were afraid to enter. But soon one imp plucked up courage and flew in. Once inside he got up to all kinds of mischief. He tripped up the Bishop, knocked down the Dean and teased the members of the choir. When he started to break the windows an angel appeared and told him to stop. The imp cheekily replied, 'Stop me if you can!' Whereupon the angel at once turned it to stone and made him sit up there forever more in the Angel Choir."

"So it's alive!" Hickory gasped.

Hugh laughed, "No, Hickory, it's just a legend. It's only a statue. Look at it, it's made of stone."

Hickory looked up again and sure enough the imp was just a carved figure like his wild man.

By now, Nathaniel had collected his tools together and joined them in the choir. He put a fatherly arm around Hickory's shoulder and smiled at him. "It's an old tale Hickory, I heard that the other imp bent the spire at Chesterfield Cathedral and escaped on a witch's broomstick only to be turned into a black cat. Forget him lad. Now, come on let's go and eat."

They all turned to leave the cathedral just as darkness descended, but as Hickory looked back one more time, he was sure the imp winked at him!

⚡

"It's alive I tell you!" Hickory was pacing up and down the tiny room as Fern tried desperately to sleep.

"But Bishop Hugh and Nathaniel said it is

just a carving," she replied impatiently. "Now go to sleep!" Fern put aside her tiny bundle of herbs knowing that they would run out tomorrow and that the *Foul Death* would grip the quarter again. Then she collapsed with exhaustion onto her straw bed, rolled over and closed her eyes.

But Hickory could not sleep and as he paced the room a plan began to formulate in his mind. It was a last desperate hope and if it failed, everyone in the quarter was very likely to die. But what if it worked? What if it worked?

⚡

Fat, heavy drops of rain fell from a leaden sky and to the inhabitants of the cathedral quarter it seemed as if God himself was trying to nail down a coffin lid upon them. It was so dark that if it weren't for the crowing of the cockerels in the market place outside the palisade, no one inside would even have realised that the night had ended and the day had come.

Yet one new inhabitant of the quarter could not wait for the dawn to break and in the smallest room of the Bishop of Lincoln's Palace, green fingers hurriedly pulled up woollen breeches and buttoned up a flaxen tunic. For Hickory was brimming with excitement. He'd hardly slept and now, as the new day began, he pulled, pushed and propelled his older sister out of her warm, comfortable bed and off through the falling rain to the cathedral.

"This had better be good!" Fern exclaimed, as her brother pushed the great doors open and half-dragged her down the nave.

Picking up a candle and marching through the half-dark chancel, Hickory led Fern until at last they stood below the tiny statue of the Lincoln Imp.

"Well, what about it?" Fern was incensed. She knew that today her healing powers would end, for the last of her herbs would be used up and now he had dragged her on some wild goose chase.

But Hickory's enthusiasm couldn't be halted and as he shone the candle up toward the statue Fern could not help but stare up at the tiny figure.

"It's still alive," Hickory whispered. "I know it is."

"I don't know," she replied. Fern was unsure. She wanted to believe her brother but the Bishop and Nathaniel had merely laughed at Hickory.

"You have to believe me, Fern," the boy's voice grew desperate. "He could be our only chance of survival."

But before Fern could ask Hickory what he meant, he rushed over to a scaffolding ladder and ran back with it. "Follow me up!" he shouted and suddenly he was up the steps and away.

Reluctantly she pursued him and moments later, in the glimmering light of the single candle, the green children looked long and hard into the imp's stone face . . . but there was nothing there, no twitch of recognition, no stirring in the blank eyes, no words from the carven lips.

"Children!" the voice bellowed down the nave and echoed around the empty cathedral. "What are you doing up there?" Nathaniel's words sang through the choir stalls as he and Bishop Hugh ran toward them.

Fern climbed down the steps and turned to greet them. "It's Hickory! He has some crazy idea that the imp is really alive," she gasped.

The Bishop and the old man laughed at the boy but Hickory looked down at them all with scorn.

"You don't understand," he said, again. "He is our only saviour, our last hope."

"You've said that already, Hickory, but

what do you mean by it?" Fern asked.

But her brother wasn't listening. He slipped his left hand into his pocket and pulled out Fern's tiny bundle of herbs.

"Why have you got those?" Nathaniel asked, "They are all that are left in the quarter."

"No more will be brought in," the Bishop added. "The quarantine guards won't allow it."

"I know!" Hickory stated, but he did not let go of them.

"But Hickory, without them many will fall to the plague," Fern's voice was full of concern, but she had never seen her brother so resolute.

"I know all of that," he spoke firmly, "but I have thought long and hard about this - you have to trust me."

"What does the boy intend to do with them?" the Bishop looked at Fern.

"I think he means to set free the imp," Fern said, guessing his intentions.

"But it's stone!" the Bishop's voice was incredulous, "and he'll destroy the herbs."

"No!" cried Fern.

But it was too late. Hickory had crushed the herbs in his hands and as he chanted the words he had heard his sister say so many times before, he threw them upon the stone figure of the imp.

The candle flickered as the fragments of herbs fluttered in the air like a gentle green rain. Below, the Bishop, Nathaniel and Fern gasped in despair as the wasted remains fell all around them, their healing powers crushed. But high above, Hickory watched in wonder as the stone came to life!

First the imp's ears twitched, then its eyes flickered, its claw-like fingers wiggled and its mouth smiled. Suddenly, it moved its legs, sat up and from behind it, small wings opened and fluttered.

As it became fully alive it stretched out its arms and then it let out a devilish cackle and swooped down right towards Hickory's face. It stopped just short of the boy's nose, glanced down and blew out the candle in Hickory's left hand. Then it gripped hold of the ladder with its tiny claws and with a chuckle, pushed it over. Hickory fell through the darkness, but Nathaniel moved to catch the boy as he tumbled down to earth. They both fell upon the cathedral floor with a bump.

The imp then darted downwards, aiming straight at Fern and Bishop Hugh. At the last moment it swerved and knocked the Bishop's hat to the floor, then it twisted in the air, stuck

out a claw, grabbed a handful of Fern's locks and gave a hard yank. As the girl cried out and the Bishop swore, the imp laughed and giggled. Finally it flew back up to its perch, where it had sat for so many years and grinned down, mischievously, at them all.

"So, how exactly is that thing going to save us?" Fern turned upon her brother as she pulled the strands of hair off her shoulder. She was angrier than Hickory had ever seen her and after the imp's devilish display, he too was beginning to doubt if his plan would work. However, he tried to speak with calm authority.

"He is going to fly out of the cathedral, over the palisade and the quarantine and off into the countryside to find fresh herbs for us. He will save this city from the plague."

At that point everyone's eyes looked up at the imp in disbelief whilst he sat there upon his perch, smiling away and picking his nose.

11: The Wild Wolves

~ A howl in the night can give you a fright ~

"What was that?" the guard on the palisade wall ducked as something flew past him.

"What was what?" his fellow militia man asked in reply.

"Something just flew past me and pinched my ear."

"It was nothing. Just the wind I expect."

"Since when did the wind have fingers?"

"Maybe it was a carrion crow, there's plenty of them down there by the pit. Perhaps it pecked you on the way," the guard laughed but then the hairs on the back of his neck stood up as a distant howling pierced the air around them.

The two men searched down along the wide, cobbled street that led down to the river. "Look!" the first guard pointed a long, bony finger to the horizon as a pack of dark, angular shapes came into view. Eyes glimmered in the torchlight and a low snarling rose from the deserted streets below.

"Let them in, perhaps they'll help to cleanse the pitiful place," the guards looked back to the tower to see the face of the Gildmaster.

They nodded in obeisance and then pulled hard on the winch that held the great door of the palisade wall. The pack of creatures quickly slipped under and the gate was dropped back into place.

"Poor devils," the guard muttered under his breath as he looked back to the houses in the plague quarter.

"As if they haven't got enough to worry about!"

At first they thought it was the wind whistling through the alleyways when they heard the howling in the Bishop's chambers, but Fern knew different. She knew it wasn't the wind but the cry of a wolf!

"I'm not surprised they've come," Bishop Hugh looked worried. "The plague pit where the dead are buried isn't deep enough. If only the militia had taken the bodies out of the quarter and buried them outside the city walls."

"I've seen foxes, dogs and even cats rooting around the corpses late at night," Brother Edmund stated, mournfully. "Now wolves, how awful!"

"Well, it's February, the Gaelic people call it the month of the ravaging wolves. I suspect hunger has driven them deeper into human territory, though they usually steer well clear of men," Bishop Hugh continued.

Nathaniel rose from his chair and looked down upon the Minster Yard. "The Vikings have a tale of a great wolf called Fenrir. He becomes so terrible that the gods decide he must be restrained. The god Tyr places a leash around Fenrir's jaws but he can only do so if he places his hand in the wolf's mouth. Fenrir bites off Tyr's hand but the magical leash, made from the most powerful things of the earth binds the wolf tight. And Fenrir is trapped until the world ends and then . . . " Nathaniel stopped speaking as another howl reverberated through the empty streets.

"And then, what?" asked Hickory.

"And then he and the other wolves will come back to swallow the earth and sky," Nathaniel finished.

"Perhaps that time has come," said Brother Edmund, who had been listening silently in the shadows of the chamber.

"No, that age is not yet." Bishop Hugh rose from his chair and knelt down by his friend and servant.

"Times are dark, Edmund, but we must have faith."

"In my homeland, wolves are a sign of

death and rebirth - good and evil," Fern interrupted and rose from the fireside to join Nathaniel by the high chamber window. "They are intelligent, powerful and untamed." Her eyes glistened as a distant recollection came back to her.

"I think we have become too far distanced from nature," Bishop Hugh answered. "What we fear, we attack and what we attack, we call evil. It doesn't really mean our enemies are evil and it might mean they are not really our enemies either. We must learn about their ways and try not to judge them from our own point of view."

"Well said, your worship." Nathaniel turned away from the window. "And we are, of course, searching for a wolf anyway," Nathaniel laughed as he spoke, "a wolf's head at least!"

"What do you mean?" Hickory looked confused.

"A wolf's head is the title given to an outlaw. Robin Hood is a wolf's head - a wanted man," Bishop Hugh finished Nathaniel's explanation for him.

"I see," Hickory replied, but before he could ask more questions cries filtered up to the Bishop's chamber. This time it wasn't the howling of the wolves but the shouts of men.

They all stared down into the streets to see a red-gold glimmer of torches, dancing in the dark like fireflies, as the townsfolk chased the pack of wolves away from the plague pit.

"Why did the militia let them in, in the first place?" Nathaniel wondered aloud.

Bishop Hugh turned to answer him with only one word, "Blackforth!"

"Father," the boy rubbed his knee and a slight trickle of blood oozed from the graze and slipped between his chubby fingers. "Father," he shouted again, but no reply came as the procession of torches he'd been following disappeared around the corner of the Minster Yard.

Suddenly, the boy was alone in the street and then he heard the noise. It was a low growling sound, a heartstopping sound and the boy knew instantly what it was. Lying there on the cobbles, he turned his head to look behind him as two wild grey eyes stared back out of the gloom. Thoughts of what to do next flashed through his young mind. Should he run? His knee stung like hell. How far could he get without the beast pouncing upon him? Or should he stay still? He knew that worked with his own dog, but then this was a wild wolf, not a lame mongrel!

The wolf edged towards him, slowly pacing around to his left, and then to his right, looking for an opening to attack. The boy stared back at the beast, taking in its huge teeth and its snarling jaws. He watched its warm breath rise in the winter air and then he closed his eyes as the beast moved in for the kill.

But the gnashing of those teeth and the snapping of those jaws never came. Instead, the boy felt another presence in the empty street and as he opened his eyes, he saw a boy standing between him and the wolf. He blinked in the starlight and then realised that the boy he was staring at was green!

Watching in silence, his mouth dropped in awe as the boy put a hand upon the wolf's snout and breathed words into its ears. Strange words, in a language the young lad upon the cobbles didn't recognise. But they were powerful words and instantly the wolf stopped growling. Its eyes turned to meet the green boy's and then it held up its head and howled into the wind. From the neighbouring street another howl echoed a reply and suddenly the wolf turned tail and darted off into the black night.

The lad on the floor tried to stand, but his knee still hurt too much and he sat back upon the cobbles.

"Where did you come from?" he said, whilst he wiped tears from his eyes and stared at the green boy in wonder.

"Oh, I was just out for an evening stroll," Hickory replied, with a wink.

"You're one of them, aren't you?" the boy shuffled back from him.

"One of what?"

"One of them creatures from the tales I've

heard. My cousin said there was a green angel saving those with the sickness and even Father told me he'd caught sight of a green boy, but I didn't believe 'em."

"Looks like you should have then," the green boy grinned.

The boy wiped his nose on his sleeve and then said, "How did you do that with the wolf?"

"Do what?" the green boy played dumb. He knew his skin colour was already enough to make people afraid of him. He didn't want them to know he could talk with wild creatures too.

The young boy stared at him for a long moment and then a raised voice cut through the awkwardness.

"Thomas!" the boy's father rounded the corner at a trot having realised his son had been left behind.

"I'm here, father," the boy shouted back as he picked himself up off the cobbles. "The wolves came for me but I'm alright, he saved me." The boy turned slowly to point at his green saviour but he'd already vanished back into the shadows!

12: Hannibal Gammon

~ You can never be sure if the water runs pure ~

By morning the wolves had gone, but Fern's worst fears were back to haunt them instead. The use of her last few precious herbs by Hickory now seemed rash as those who had not yet fully recovered from the disease quickly fell back under its deathly spell. Will Scarlet's progress halted too and he slipped back into semi-consciousness. Worse still, new outbreaks arose all around the quarter and the sickness sprang up again like a weed.

Outside the palisade walls however, one man rubbed his hands in glee, as orders for his useless plague remedies doubled. In fact it was proving to be a very good day all round for Giles Blackforth. Not only was his apothecary business back up and running, but he'd just discovered that an old rival was being blamed for this fresh outbreak.

"So, they think Aaron the Jew has been poisoning everyone do they? Fantastic!" he muttered to himself as the guard took the crate of potions and handed the Gildmaster a leather bag full of clinking silver pennies,

The men and women outside the

moneylender's house were angry and aggressive but most of all they were frightened. For many of them, last night's attack by the wolf pack had been the last straw. Watching their families die had been bad enough, but to see remnants of their loved one's clothing strewn across the cobbles and to catch sight of flesh and bone left out in the street by the ravaging wolves had finally driven them to despair. A sudden need to exact vengeance on someone suddenly overwhelmed the good people of Lincoln.

"They have brought it from abroad!" a woman screamed out.

"They killed our Lord and saviour," shouted another, as she held a child's dress in her hand.

"The Jew is trying to murder us all!" a fat man shouted, his cry echoing through the narrow streets outside the home of Aaron the Jew.

Under the eaves of the shop, halfway down Steep Hill, a mob now gathered. Grey were their faces in the morning light; worn and withered. Many of them had lost sons or daughters, fathers or husbands, mothers or wives to this dreaded disease and now, whipped up into a rage, their grief burst forward. Their shouts and cries woke the rest of the quarter and inside the moneylender's house, the shutters were suddenly opened in the upstairs window.

As the early morning sun slipped behind the brooding clouds in shame, the wooden door, so intricately carved with the proud owner's design, was shattered open as the mob charged at it with a pew stolen from the cathedral. Wooden splinters from both the door and the bench bit into the rabble like a thousand miniature sword thrusts, but their blood was up and they ignored their pain in a frenzy of retribution.

Then, moments after the door had been broken, the sad sight of Aaron appeared in the gaping doorway. Dressed in only his nightgown, he was knocked to the floor in a flurry of fists and then howls of hatred filled the street as he was dragged over the cobbles by his curly black hair.

In the chambers of the Bishop's palace, Fern and Hickory heard the din before anyone else and they ran out into the morning light to see what was happening. The Bishop and Nathaniel were hot on their heels and as they all crossed the Minster Yard, the Bishop's assistant, Brother Edmund, came running the other way.

"What on earth is happening, Edmund?"

the Bishop held the priest's arms as he ran toward them.

"A mob has broken into the moneylender's house," he gasped.

"Who's the ringleader?"

"Hannibal Gammon!" Edmund spat out the name.

"I might well have guessed," Hugh replied.

"Who's he?" asked Nathaniel.

"A silversmith, although he seems to have his ample fingers in a number of pies," the Bishop looked down the hill anxiously. "He's also high up in the gilds, second only to Giles Blackforth himself."

"He's rotten to the core," Edmund interrupted.

"Now Edmund, let's not be too uncharitable."

"You see the good in everyone, your worship, but what they're doing to that poor Jewish merchant is unholy."

"Yes, you're quite right and we don't have time to gossip. Let's away!" and they all followed the Bishop across the square.

◌⃰

Initially, Hannibal Gammon had profited well from the *Foul Death*. A fortune was to be made from selling the silver dust that folk believed stopped the plague entering your house, if you sprinkled it liberally outside your front door. Of course Gammon helped spread this belief and the fact that he had plenty of the dust lying around his workshop was just pure coincidence. If it hadn't been for the intervention of Giles Blackforth, his Gild superior, he'd have cornered the market, but Blackforth swiftly took control of the lucrative business, until the people of Lincoln grew wise to its ineffectiveness.

When Gammon's own wife, Rosie, fell foul of the disease, he did what every loving husband would do - he left her to die while he moved in with his colleague next door! There was no denying he loved his wife, but he couldn't risk catching the plague himself. When he finally gained courage to go and visit her, he found her already dead. It was at that point he looked for someone to blame and it was why he now led the mob that stood howling outside the Jew's door.

"Throw him down the well!" a tall man holding a blacksmith's hammer shouted.

"Good idea, he's the one who poisoned it," replied Gammon, and he grabbed old Aaron by the scruff of the neck and hauled him down to the well at the bottom of Steep Hill.

"I feared this would happen," Bishop Hugh

spoke quickly, as they turned the corner of the Minster Yard and caught sight of the mob.

"What do you mean?" Hickory asked.

"It was inevitable that at some point the blame would fall upon the Jews. It always has. From York to Southampton, in times of trouble, the Jewish quarter is the first to be attacked. Only the French are more hated than the Jews!"

"This is your fault, Hickory!" Fern turned upon her brother, still angry that he'd wasted her herbs.

"I'm sorry," he replied. "I thought it was for the best."

"There's no time to argue about that now," Nathaniel intervened and put a hand on Hickory's shoulder. "We must save your friend, Aaron."

"Let him go!" Hickory hollered as he ran through the crowd and grabbed a hold of Aaron's nightshirt in a desperate attempt to stop the old man from being thrown down the well. But as Hickory held tight to Aaron he felt strong muscular hands grab hold of him.

"Get out of here!" Hannibal Gammon shouted into the boy's face, as he ordered two of his henchmen to take the boy away. But Hickory was determined not to let go of his friend and he gripped hard as the old man was pushed toward the edge of the well.

"Right, chuck him down too! "Gammon ordered, as he turned toward Hickory. "He's just a green freak anyway."

The mob, caught up in the fervour of the moment shouted their agreement and suddenly both Aaron and Hickory were lifted high above the gaping hole by a number of outstretched hands. Fern, Nathaniel and the Bishop, stuck at the back of the crowd, found themselves unable to break through the chaos.

But then, right down by the side of the well, a young boy's high-pitched voice sang out and all eyes turned to see a grubby faced lad of no more than six push past everyone and run to stand next to Hannibal Gammon, "He saved me from the wolves," the boy said, as he pointed a stubby finger towards Hickory.

"It's true," said a bulky figure wearing a butcher's apron as he followed the young boy through the mob and put a hand on his son's shoulder. "Thomas told me all about it." The man carried a large butcher's knife in his hand and had a look on his face that dared the mob to question him. A sudden hush descended upon them all. "You all know me," he continued, "you know my word can be trusted."

"Ulfgar the butcher doesn't lie," a voice from the back of the crowd agreed and a general mumbling reverberated around the streets.

"But the Jew's poisoned the water and this green brat has appeared when we have all been suffering," Gammon exclaimed, as the mood of the crowd slowly turned against him.

"But there's nothing wrong with the water, Hannibal," Hugh spoke calmly as he made his way to the front of the silent crowd. He took a long look at the faces around him and then he strode across to the well and dropped the bucket down into the blackness. It fell twenty feet and then there was a splash! Then he hurriedly pulled on the winch and the rope bobbed up and down like a fisherman's line until the bucket reappeared full of water. Quickly, he gathered in the rope, grabbed the bucket and held it high so all the crowd could see what he was up to.

"Don't do it!" a voice sounded out, but Hugh ignored the cry, smiled and took a swig of the well-water.

Many in the crowd gasped, fully expecting to see their Bishop turn and stagger to the floor - poisoned. But when he didn't, all eyes turned back upon Gammon and his cronies.

"Delicious!" said Hugh, as he put the bucket down. "Proof, I believe, that Aaron is innocent of trying to murder us all. Now, I think you should apologise and let him go," the Bishop stared at the silversmith. But Gammon had gone too far to back down now.

"No, I won't apologise! If it isn't the well-water, then he's murdering us all by some other means. Perhaps he sends this little green devil into our houses at night." He glared, angrily, at Hickory. "That's how he does it, I'll bet. He probably killed your families that way," Gammon's face searched the crowd for support. "I'd put money on it that that's how he murdered my Rosie!"

"How would you know?" a woman's voice growled back bitterly from the mob, "You weren't with her when she died!"

"Yeah, you'd already scarpered and left the poor dear to suffer alone," another woman echoed the first.

The silversmith's round face turned scarlet in a combination of rage and embarrassment and suddenly, as Hickory and Aaron were lowered to safety, Gammon drew a knife from his belt and charged toward Hickory. But as he did so a small creature shot past his ear and pulled the blade from his grip. In a swirl of hands and tiny wings the knife went spinning down into the well. It scraped along the stone sides and then fell into the water with a harmless splash.

Hands now grabbed hard upon the bulky girth of Hannibal Gammon and, as he screamed in rage, all eyes glanced upwards in wonder, as a soft, green rain seemed to fall down upon them.

"I knew it," said Hickory, as he smiled skywards.

"Knew what?" asked Fern, as she rushed to put her arms around her brother.

"I knew he'd come back," he said, as he pointed to the sky.

13: The Healing Time

~ Do not judge heroes by their reputation ~

A tiny figure, about the size of a bat, danced about in the sky above them and from a linen sack it threw out handfuls of green leaves, which fluttered down to the cobbled streets, filling the air with a sweet aroma.

"Herbs!" cried Fern, as she suddenly realised what the green rain was. "How wonderful. He's found herbs!"

She was right of course. The creature that now flew down to perch upon the top of the well had indeed been throwing down handfuls of herbs. Leaves of wood sorrell, borage and scented hairhood fell with sprigs of thyme, sage and rosemary. Fern quickly scooped them all up. The imp grinned at her mischievously and threw her the linen sack. She caught it deftly and as she looked inside and saw more herbs, as well as the roots and seeds of useful plants, her face beamed with optimism. "Now we can finally cure this *Foul Death!*" she shouted, and everyone looked toward her with hope.

"She's right!" stated Hugh. "We all know the skills this young lady has with healing and now our own imp has returned with herbs to save the day." The crowd by the well stared at the imp who stood up on the winch and bowed to them all. Smiles broke amongst the grim faces, many grinned back at the tiny figure and some of the children laughed out aloud.

"Now," Hugh continued, "I suggest we all return to our homes and in due course we will visit the sick and hopefully turn the tide of this terrible disease."

"What shall we do with him?" Ulfgar the butcher pushed Hannibal Gammon forward.

"Well, he's done no real harm," Hugh replied, as he looked upon the silversmith. "I hope you have learned something here today, Hannibal. Now return home and make good your wrongdoings."

"And how exactly will I do that?" Gammon eyed the Bishop with contempt.

"You will assist Fern and I in administering help to the sick."

"What, enter the houses of those with the plague?" Gammon was incredulous.

"I mean exactly that, Hannibal."

The crowd stared at the fat silversmith with a mixture of guilt, on account of their own part in the proceedings, and righteousness over the punishment involved. Then, silently, they made their way back to their houses and in minutes the street was empty.

"Thank you," Aaron straightened his nightshirt and smiled down at Hickory. "You risked your life for me and I will not forget that."

"Us strangers have to stick together," Hickory grinned.

"If only we all stuck together, then there wouldn't be any strangers," Nathaniel muttered thoughtfully whilst he took a cloth from his belt and wiped mud from Hickory's face.

"Come along then, Aaron," Hugh put an arm around the old Jew's shoulder and he and Brother Edmund walked him slowly back to his shop. Behind them Fern threw the sack of herbs over her shoulder and followed Nathaniel and Hickory back to the Bishop's palace and above them the imp flew high above the rooftops, enjoying his freedom. A white shaft of winter sun split the dark clouds like a silver sword and glanced off his flapping wings, illuminating him like a messenger from heaven.

"Look!" exclaimed Hickory, as he watched the white-silver dot cross the sky. "He looks more like an angel than a devil."

Nathaniel smiled at the sight and then at

Hickory. "We must all show faith like yours, it seems, if we really want miracles." And then they all laughed out loudly as the imp flew out of the sunlight and down to the palisade wall, where he promptly kicked one of the guards up the backside and disappeared from view.

᠀

And so Fern worked her 'magic'. 'Tree magic' the people called it, though to her it was only knowledge of how to use the gifts of the wild: an inborn skill that all her people knew. She and Hugh, with Hannibal Gammon carrying the precious remedies behind them, worked day and night. Slowly they did indeed turn the tide of the sickness and life gradually flowed back into the cathedral quarter.

By the end of the week the streets were full again. Market stalls rose up in the Minster Yard and supplies came over the palisade walls at last. And then, in a strange twist of fate, Hannibal Gammon failed to appear one morning and when Bishop Hugh and Brother Edmund entered his house, they discovered him slumped in his bed, lying close to death.

"Just desserts, I'd say," Edmund looked down upon the shivering silversmith with little sympathy.

"Come now, Edmund. He's paid his dues with the help he's given Fern and I these past few days."

"I suppose so, your worship, but there is a sense of irony in it, don't you think?"

"Perhaps, but I would not let anyone fall if they could be saved, Edmund, in body or soul."

"Yes, you are right, your worship, and I'll fetch the girl to help him."

And help him she did! In fact, by the following day there were no new cases of the *'Foul Death'* reported anywhere in the cathedral quarter and that night the Black Bull Inn re-opened and a feast took place inside. John and Katherine Rathbone laid on a wonderful spread and by the time Bishop Hugh and Brother Edmund entered the tavern it was already in full swing.

"Scarlet's on the mend and with any luck might be well enough to talk by morning," the Bishop had to shout the news to Nathaniel and the children as the chatter around the feasting table got more and more raucous.

"I'll drink to that!" exclaimed Nathaniel, as he held his tankard up high.

"Me too," said Hickory, as he clinked his own against Nathaniel's and grinned with enthusiasm. He had never tried ale before!

"Not too much now, lad." Nathaniel eyed Hickory carefully as he took a swig of the beer.

"Wow!" he said, as he wiped white froth from his lips. "That tastes good."

"Look at him," Fern laughed, as she watched a small shape jump up from his seat and skip along the bench.

"Guest of honour, hey?" Bishop Hugh watched the tiny figure with amusement. "Not bad for a little devil," and they all chuckled when the Lincoln Imp juggled apples and pears whilst he danced upon the table.

Whilst he jigged up and down, Ulfgar the butcher and two other tradesmen started to croon a local song and before long the whole inn was singing merrily along to the tune of the Lincolnshire Poacher:

The Lincolnshire Poacher

When I was bound apprentice in famous Lincolnshire,
Full well I served my master for more than seven years.
Till I took up the poaching as you shall quickly hear,
Oh, 'tis my delight on a shiny night in the season of
the year.

As me and my companions were setting off a snare,
'Twas then we saw the gamekeeper for him we did
not care.

For we can wrestle and we can fight and jump out
    anywhere,
Oh, 'tis my delight on a shiny night in the season of
    the year.

I threw the hare on my shoulder and then we all
    trudged home,
We took him to the butcher's shop and sold him for
    a crown.
We sold him for a crown my lads, but I didn't tell
    you where,
Oh, 'tis my delight on a shiny night in the season of
    the year.

Success to every nobleman that lives in Lincolnshire,
Success to every poacher that wants to sell a hare.
Bad luck to every gamekeeper that will not sell his
    deer,
Oh, 'tis my delight on a shiny night in the season of
    the year.

As the singing subsided the door of the inn
was flung open and a small boy came flying
through the door. Hickory turned to see
young Thomas, the boy he'd saved from the
wolves, come stumbling through the crowd.

"You got lost again?" his father laughed.

"No, father, I've got news."

"Well, what is it boy?" The inn grew silent
and all eyes turned to the youngster.

"It's over, the quarantine's over. Tomorrow
the gates of the palisade will finally be open!"
and then the little lad's voice was lost amongst
the cheers!

14: Flight Into Darkness

~ Not all the creatures of the sky can fly ~

The palisade gates creaked open to huge shouts of approval and great sighs of relief. It had been almost three months since the quarantine had been enforced and many families had been split asunder by the division. Husbands and sons, away trading, now stood searching for their loved ones in the gateway. Uncles and brothers, who worked the barge boats along the River Witham, rushed forth. Cousins, sisters, grandparents and friends of those trapped inside all flocked forward to see who had survived the dark days of the disease.

There were tears of joy for those relatives who found their kin still alive, but there were tears of sadness too for those that nobody ran to embrace. All that was left for them was a red cross on a doorway and a sorry glance at the plague pit, where one old woman stood alone and desolate. She had been a mother and a grandmother and now she was nothing but an old widow. A beloved son, a doting daughter-in-law and two beautiful grandchildren all now lay cold in the ground before her feet.

But there was happiness too. A tall woman with long black hair and olive skin ran to meet a well-dressed figure standing by the gate. "Shalom," the man said, in Hebrew, as she stroked the bruises upon his smiling face. "It's good to have you home, Rachel," Aaron the Jew said, as he kissed his daughter on the forehead.

Returning from her mother's house in York, Alewith, the butcher's wife, looked around anxiously for her husband and son. Then she heard a familiar voice and she cried with joy as Thomas' grubby face appeared through the crowd. He ran into her outstretched arms and Ulfgar followed close behind him. He embraced his wife and the three of them walked hand in hand through the throng and made their way back to their shop.

While the joys and the tragedies of the reunion played out by the palisade gate, high up in his chamber Will Scarlet's eyes at last blinked open. "Good morning, Will," Bishop Hugh took Scarlet's hand in his own and wiped his brow with a damp cloth. "These people have helped you to recover and now they in turn need your help," he said, as he pointed to the children.

"What do they want? " Scarlet's voice croaked with lack of use.

"Do you know of Robin Hood?" Nathaniel asked gently.

Scarlet looked anxious and for many moments said nothing. "Why on earth would I know of an infamous Wolf's Head!" he finally said, with feigned indignation.

"It's okay, Will," the Bishop reassured him, "they know who you really are."

Scarlet closed his eyes, deep in thought, and then opened them again and as he did so a ray of light seemed to shine from them as he remembered times past. Then he turned toward them all and smiled. "Okay," he admitted, "of course I know of Robin Hood. I lived and fought with him for many years."

"Can you tell us where we can find him, please?" Nathaniel bent close to the old outlaw.

"In his forest, of course, deep in the heart of Sherwood," Scarlet coughed and Fern passed him a mug of water. He gulped down a mouthful and wiped his chin. "Thank you," he spluttered, staring at Fern with eyes open wide in wonder.

"How will we find him?" Nathaniel continued his gentle probing.

"If you make it as far as Sherwood, then he will find you!" Scarlet smiled sleepily and turned his head upon the pillow.

"Is he green like us?" Hickory interrupted, but no answer came as the outlaw slipped back into unconsciousness.

"Ask him later," Nathaniel said softly, aware of the boy's impatience.

But there was to be no later, as a sudden cry outside caught them unawares. They rushed to the chamber window and stared down at the palisade gateway to see a line of militia guards push their way through the crowds. At the head of the men-at-arms a tall figure barked orders at the soldiers. "Giles Blackforth!" Bishop Hugh stared at the figure with concern. "What's he up to?" he wondered aloud.

A fat figure ran across the Minster Yard and bowed in front of Blackforth. He spoke to the Gildmaster at pace and then with a chubby finger, Hannibal Gammon pointed up toward them at the chamber window. In horror, they all watched as Blackforth followed his gaze. Catching sight of the faces peering down at him, Blackforth turned to his militiamen and gave instructions. Within moments, the men-at-arms had pulled their swords from their scabbards and were racing up toward the townhouse.

"Quickly! You must run, children. It's clear Blackforth has come for you and I doubt I will be able to stop him." Hugh pushed Nathaniel and the children to the doorway. "Brother Edmund and I will try to delay them for as long as possible."

"Thank you for all you have done for us," said Fern holding the Bishop's hand tightly. "It is I that should be thanking you. But we have no time for that now. Go!" Hugh relinquished her hand as he and Edmund ran down the stairs to meet the guards.

Nathaniel, Fern and Hickory listened briefly whilst Hugh argued with the men below and then they climbed out of the window and escaped across the rooftops.

᪥

"There they are!" the shout alerted the guards as three figures scrambled across the slates and clambered onto the stonemason's scaffolding that lay straddled against the cathedral roof. "Get up there after them," the voice of the Gildmaster bellowed across the square, as all eyes turned upward.

Suddenly, a vicious wind cut across the quarter and a steady shower of snow began to fall. Fat, white flakes fell upon the soldiers who charged back across the Minster Yard and pushed aside the protesting townsfolk who viewed Fern and Hickory as their saviours.

For a brief moment Nathaniel and the children were unsure of what to do, as the line of soldiers followed them up the scaffolding.

"Look there," Hickory grabbed hold of the old man's arm and pointed to a small, open window, on the south side of the nave. "They haven't refitted the stained glass yet. Do you think you can squeeze through?"

Nathaniel took a hard look at the narrow opening, regretting the feast he'd scoffed the night before. "We have no other choice, but it's best if you two go first just in case I get stuck," he gasped, as the snow blew into his face.

Carefully, they sped to the window and one by one they squeezed through. Nathaniel was pulled inside and he landed with a bump, only for Hickory to pull him up and shove a bundle of black material into his arms. "Here, take these and follow me," he exclaimed and before he and Fern could ask what the boy had in mind he was out the door.

They left the tiny room to find themselves high up in the gallery on the inside of the cathedral. Behind them they heard groans as the following soldiers squeezed through the window. Below them, on the floor of the nave, they watched in dismay as more guards spilled inside.

But Hickory had a plan and as he led Fern and Nathaniel ever upward he grinned at his sister and the old man. "What's he up to?" Nathaniel looked at Fern with scepticism as Hickory handed them wooden poles and a ball of rope that he'd discovered by a cluster of workman's tools.

"Nearly there," Hickory exclaimed, as he opened a tiny door in the far corner of the gallery. "Come on you two! They're gaining on us!" He was right. The men-at arms, swords gripped tightly, came charging around the corner. Fern screamed as an arrow bit into the wood of the pole she held, an inch away from her face. Then a spear flew across the narrow landing and took the nose off a statue of the blessed Saint Barnabus! Pushing Nathaniel through the door, Hickory slammed it shut and then wedged one of his poles up against the handle. "It won't hold them for long," he puffed. "Now, up that ladder!"

While they climbed up through the slender passageway, statues toppled all around them and chunks of uncarved stone plummeted downwards in chaos. Hurriedly they rushed up the last few rungs of the ladder and scrambled out through another door to find themselves on top of the cathedral roof. Below them they heard the door splinter open with a crash, and a flurry of shouts signalled that the soldiers were still in hot pursuit.

Outside, on the rooftop, an icy blast of wind met them. It whipped at their faces whilst wet snow fell like white rain, freezing on the cold stone parapets in an instant. As they looked down at the Minster Yard far below, the watching crowd seemed like tiny specks and they suddenly became aware that they were hundreds of feet above the ground. Quickly, they clambered over a pile of mason's tools and rushed to the far side of the roof. Under their feet, a thin layer of ice glimmered like glass upon the slate tiles and they slipped and slid dangerously close to the edge as they ran!

Behind them, the first man-at-arms had already made it up the ladder, but as he pursued them, he lost his footing on the treacherous tiles and tumbled over the side of the roof with a clatter. A blood-curdling scream rang out, as the soldier fell three hundred feet to the snowy ground below.

But other men now appeared! Nathaniel and the children dodged behind the great spire and stood with their backs firm against the cold stone. Hickory grabbed the black material that he'd handed to Nathaniel and gasped, "What are these cloaks called?"

"Why, they're cassocks - priests' robes. That room must have been the vestry where the priests got changed," the old man answered.

"Right, well watch what I do and spread the cassocks across the wooden poles."

Fern and Nathaniel stared at each other with puzzled expressions as Hickory held the end of the poles in his hands and stretched his arms out wide like a bat. "Now, tie the ends to my wrists with the rope and then I'll do yours," he shouted, as he looked up to the sky.

"You're not planning what I think you're planning are you?" Nathaniel grabbed the boy by the arm as he started to move away from their hiding place.

"Oh, no, Hickory!" Fern had also guessed what her brother had in mind.

The boy turned back and smiled at the two of them. "Do you have a better idea?" he shouted through the wind. "Now, follow me!" and with that he stepped out from the shadows of the spire.

The militia men spotted them straight away and drew back their bowstrings, but hampered by the wind and the snow their shafts bounced harmlessly off the statues around the escaping figures and with Hickory leading, the three of them ran quickly to the edge of the roof.

"This is madness!" Nathaniel cried through the swirling snow.

"I know," replied Fern.

"Trust me," shouted Hickory, and he spread his arms out wide.

Suddenly, an arrow ripped through the cloth of his makeshift wing and as he turned, he watched in horror as three soldiers drew back their bows again. Hickory closed his eyes, waiting for the expected shafts to find their mark, but then from nowhere a tiny figure appeared and darted around the men pulling their hair, tripping their ankles and knocking their weapons to the floor. The soldiers tried, in vain, to catch the creature. Two of them lost their grip upon the slates and slipped to the floor, hugging the tiles for dear life. The third cursed as the beast knocked his bow from his hand and then he crashed into a weathervane.

Nathaniel and the children relaxed for a brief moment until a scream howled out from nowhere. "You won't escape me!" a tall figure charged across the icy roof, a black and gold cloak swirling in the wind like an angry tornado. He caught hold of Fern's ankle and she cried out in terror as she looked upon the enraged face of Giles Blackforth, himself. "I've got you now," he hollered. But then the imp appeared again and with all its might it shoved a ladder towards the Gildmaster.

Blackforth threw up his arms to stop it crashing down upon him and as he did so Fern managed to scramble clear. The Gildmaster stumbled back with the impact of the ladder, but somehow he managed to knock it away. Regaining his balance, Blackforth was about to grab at Fern again, but as the ladder was sent spinning over the side his cloak became caught up in its rungs. Suddenly, just as a smile reappeared on his face, he was pulled backwards over the edge with a scream. He flung out his arms in desperation and for a brief moment his fingers gripped upon the edge of the tiles, his silver rings glinting against the ice. And then he was gone!

Whilst Nathaniel pulled Fern to her feet, the imp circled above Hickory and then swooped low. "You have saved us again," Hickory grinned at his fiendish friend, but the imp didn't answer him - he just winked and then the tiny creature flew off into the snowstorm, giggling.

"Quickly!" the boy shouted as more black shapes appeared by the spire. Then, one by one, Hickory, Fern and Nathaniel stretched

out their wings and stepped off the rooftop!

The wind caught under their wings, the cassocks billowed and they flew high into the air and across the Minster Yard. Far below them, Bishop Hugh and Brother Edmund waved frantically and a cheer echoed in the streets. They crossed over the palisade wall with a sigh of relief, but then the wind drew in its breath and for a moment there was an eerie silence. And then, they fell. Slowly at first and then faster and faster and down, down, down . . . into the darkness!

Robin Hood in Sherwood Stood

Medieval Nottinghamshire

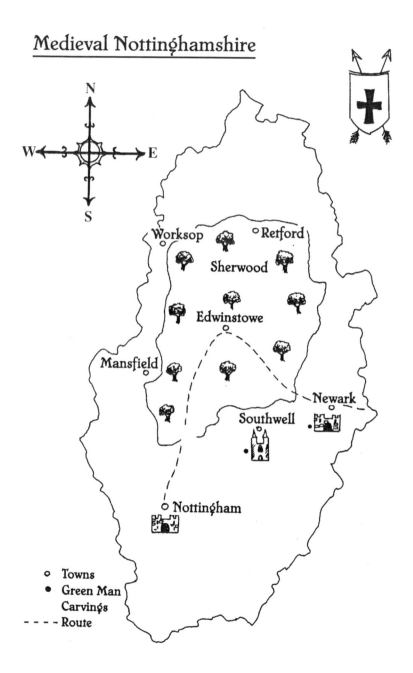

N
W — E
S

Worksop Retford
Sherwood
Edwinstowe
Mansfield
Newark
Southwell
Nottingham

○ Towns
● Green Man
Carvings
- - - - Route

15: Sherwood

~ In the Shire Wood, the men are brave and good ~

Tiny droplets of water dripped steadily onto the forest floor as the long-awaited thaw finally melted away the snows of Sherwood. On the ground, squirrels and hedgehogs meekly emerged from their hiding places as the faint rays of a pale, spring sunshine drifted lazily though the branches of the skeletal trees. From behind a knot of tall grasses a red deer peered out from the cover of those trees and searched the skyline for its mate, but then it sprinted back into the shadows as a voice echoed across the fields.

"The wind's changing," Nathaniel called out, as he watched a magpie catch the breeze and slip behind a cluster of rushing clouds, "it's coming from the west," he muttered, as he followed Fern and Hickory over a stretch of wide meadowland and onward to the great Forest of Sherwood.

At the edge of the trees, Fern looked to the sky too, but she was pensive and stood quite still for a brief moment, closing her eyes in thought. Then she spoke quietly as if still in a dream. "The east wind we call 'Escaroth'," she half-whispered, "it means 'the biting teeth', as it's hard and bitter. The south wind we call 'Tanis', the swallow's breath, soft, gentle and warm and the north wind is 'Hungarth,' the 'snowbearer'." She paused for a moment as she searched through the dark recesses of her mind. "But I can't remember the name for the west wind," her face grew sad and she turned away. "My memory's like the wind," she spoke as if to herself, "sometimes strong, at other times barely a breeze, but always it's something I cannot hold onto!"

Nathaniel stroked the girl's face and saw the worry slip away as she looked into the shadows of the forest and hope was rekindled. "Well, now we've made it here," he said, "but before we go any further along this path, I could do with a drink and something to eat. The problem is, we're out of bread and I can't see a stream!"

"We don't need a stream of water to quench our thirst," said Fern and she slipped away from the path and approached a line of tall birch trees. Delicately, she cut through the silvery bark into the trunk of one of them and proceeded to make a clean circular hole. Then, she seemed to search the floor for something and suddenly her eyes spotted what she was looking for and she knelt down and picked up a large oak leaf. Next, she went back to the old man and asked him for his leather water bottle.

"But it's empty!" Nathaniel said, looking perplexed.

"Precisely," she answered and smiled at him knowingly. Nathaniel was bemused, but he dug deep and gave her the bottle. Fern returned to the birch tree, bent the leaf in two and gently pushed it into the hole she had made in the trunk. To Nathaniel's amazement, a soft trickle of birch sap ran down the leaf and as Fern put the open bottle to the bottom edge of the leaf, a steady flow of the draft filled it up.

Once it was full, Fern took the leaf out and pushed in the wood she had earlier cut out to block up the hole again. She patted the tree, as if to say thank you, and handed the now full bottle to Nathaniel.

"Try it," she said to him.

"Are you sure?" Nathaniel had never tasted tree sap before and he wasn't entirely convinced it was safe.

"It's full of goodness!" Hickory shouted from behind him. "Go on, don't be scared!"

Nathaniel put his mouth to the bottle and took a small tentative sip. The sap tasted surprisingly sweet and he licked his lips and gulped at it.

"Not too much now," Fern berated, "it's filling and we all need some."

"Wonderful!" Nathaniel wiped his lips and gave the bottle to Fern. "But what about something to eat?"

"Wait here," she replied. And before Nathaniel could speak, the two children disappeared into the undergrowth.

Nathaniel sat down by the birch, took another gulp of the sap and waited.

Within just a few minutes both Hickory and Fern appeared from the foliage with arms full of wild sustenance. "Right, old man!" Hickory grinned. "Get ready for a woodland feast."

Before his eyes, on platters of oak leaves, the children served their forest fare. There was a salad of lime tree leaves, pink crab-apple blossom, white wild garlic buds and the five starred blue of borage flowers, dotted like jewels on an array of wild greens. There were the young leaves of lady's mantle, purifying burdock and some wood sorrel with its sharp but delicate taste. Finally, with the nutty flavoured hawthorn shoots that some call bread and cheese and the aromatic tang of shepherd's purse, there was enough to feed them all.

The wild greens were at their best and although, in truth, Nathaniel would have preferred a leg of roast mutton, they provided a real spring tonic for the old man. He looked at the children and saw the grey pallor leave their faces and a new freshness of life enter them. Fern, in particular, looked alive again and it warmed his eyes to see new life breathed into her; he knew the trials in Lincoln had been really difficult for her!

"That's better," he stated, as he lay back in the shade of the birch tree and closed his eyes. Whilst Hickory disappeared into the trees to explore, Fern sat down next to the old man and started to gently sing.

> Enameo o'tialso
> > Ai eranimo O'calso
> Tor mai tuvalu
> > Cal mar masalu

"It's a lovely song, Fern. Is it about something very beautiful?" Nathaniel asked, his eyes half-closed in a daydream.

"It's about the flowers, so yes, it is beautiful. I'll sing it in your words," she said, and then she sang once more.

> The flowers of the wood
> > sing of days that are good,
> But they forget the tale of life
> > of days of sadness and strife.

The flowers of the glade
    sing of light under shade,
But when their petals touch the ground
    weeping is their sound.

And the flowers of the meadow
    lose their voices on the breeze,
So the most beautiful song of all
    is from the flowers of the trees.

"All the flowers have a meaning as well as many uses, you know." Fern picked a small white flower and handed it to Nathaniel as she finished singing.

"I see," he said curiously, "so what about this wood anaemie?"

"It represents abandonment."

"Oh," replied the old man, "and that orchid?" he pointed to a purple flower that poked up through the anaemies.

"Loss," Fern replied, forlornly.

"Ah!" This is not going very well, Nathaniel thought. He lowered his eyes to the ground and spied a tiny white flower and picked it. He studied the fragile petals of the daisy, but was almost too scared to ask the girl what it stood for.

"It stands for hope, Nathaniel," she read his

thoughts and he handed the delicate flower to her. "Good, then perhaps that should be the emblem of our quest."

"A fine idea," Fern said, taking the daisy and pushing it into her flaxen hair. Then she knelt down and washed her face in the morning dew under the birch tree.

"Make a wish as you wash, that was a saying of my mother," Nathaniel grinned, as the girl looked up fresh faced.

Fern smiled and made her wish and then she and the old man rested back against the trunk of the birch again.

❧

A quarter of an hour later Hickory returned from his explorations to find the two of them half-asleep under the branches of the tree.

"Come on sleepy-heads!" he laughed, as he bounded out of the bushes and back into the glade. "Let's follow the badger trail, it's sure to take us through the forest safely - they are so wise."

Nathaniel watched as Hickory laid his nose down to the mossy ground and stared in wonder as the boy sniffed the floor.

"I have it," he grinned excitedly, "the scent of the track! And see here, Nathaniel," Hickory pointed at some claw marks on a fallen beech tree, "badger claws!"

The old man stared downward as Hickory marked out the four long scratches of the badger's paw and then the smallest of its five claws, which made a mark almost like a human thumb. Below the marks, Hickory found a patch of gnawed bluebell bulbs and a half chewed fern leaf that further signalled the badger's presence. He studied the leaf carefully and touched the chewed end. "It's still wet, which means the badgers were here only a few hours ago."

Nathaniel was impressed. It was clear that the skills of healing with herbs and plants that Fern possessed were matched by her brother's knowledge of the tracks and the ways of the woods.

"A deer has passed this way also. Look," Hickory pointed to two little divots in the grass. "It's kicked those up in flight. Something startled it."

"And here," added Fern, as she picked up a strand of coarse hair and handed it to Nathaniel, "it's shedding its thicker winter coat, preparing for summer."

"Now, look at this", Hickory knelt down and studied the floor.

"What is it?" Nathaniel asked.

"A sign."

"But it's just a broken branch , isn't it?" the old man saw nothing of interest.

"No, he's right," Fern knelt down next to her brother.

"Someone is using this track regularly."

"Look here," Hickory pointed at the branch to show Nathaniel that it had been twisted in a certain way.

"I've heard that the travelling peoples, who some call *Egypsies*, use a secret sign language using leaves and grass. I believe it's called *Patrin*." The old man studied the branch carefully.

"Well, I don't know if these are left by Egypsies but I do know that we can read them and that means we can find our way through this Shire Wood." Hickory rose from the hidden path and looked ahead for more secret signs.

"It also means that whoever is using them knows the hidden ways of the woods. Perhaps this Robin Hood really is . . ." Fern's voice stopped, abruptly.

"What now?" whispered Nathaniel.

"Hide! Someone's coming!" Hickory called back as he and Fern dived into the undergrowth and the old man quickly followed close behind.

16: The Hunting Party
~ The deer run quick when the huntsman beats his stick ~

From behind a cover of elder trees the old man and the children saw a black banner rippling in the air. It was held above a flurry of horsemen and looked like a swooping raven. As Nathaniel stared at the pennant he caught a glimpse of a silver device upon it, which looked like a castle. He racked his brain, trying desperately to remember whose coat-of-arms it was, but nothing came.

What was quickly apparent was that this was a hunting party, for the stag the pack were pursuing suddenly broke from the trees and jumped clean over Nathaniel and the children. Their eyes followed the deer as it disappeared into the bushes and then they looked back to the horsemen. "Quickly," Hickory said, "follow me!" and the boy bent low, slipping under the overhanging elder branches and breaking away from the path. But as Nathaniel followed him, he cracked his head on one of the branches and fell to the floor. The horsemen were almost upon them and as Fern turned back to help Nathaniel, Hickory realised that his sister and the old man were sitting targets. He sprang back out of the bushes and hollered at the approaching hunters, "Catch me if you can!" and then he ran back down the badger's trail, away from the others, as hooves thundered behind him and voices shouted out in pursuit.

Darting under low branches and hurdling over fallen trunks, Hickory ran at a great speed, but the horsemen quickly gained ground and suddenly arrows whizzed through the air around him. He put on a spurt as the shafts ripped through the leaves, but then found a woodland stream before him. He had no choice but to jump into the rushing waters, with the aim of scrambling across the slippery stones to the other side. But a searing pain suddenly tore through his calf and he looked down to find the shaft of an arrow had nipped his leg. Red blood swirled in the shallows of the stream and he stumbled. He put out his hand in front of him and closed his eyes. Huntsmen's cries were all around him, he went tumbling into the cold water and then everything went black!

᥆ᤄ

Far behind her brother, Fern hovered in the shadows like a phantom. Not all of the hunters had followed Hickory and now a soldier circled around her and the old man.

She knew she couldn't outrun the man and besides, she wouldn't leave Nathaniel behind. So, she looked around for something to defend herself with and her eyes sparkled as she saw something useful. But it wasn't a bright shining spear or a hefty sword that had caught her eye - it was a plant!

She wrapped the hem of her dress around her hand and grabbed the stalk of a giant hogweed. Careful to stay in the shade, she held the plant steady and waited for the man-at-arms to make his move. Breathlessly, she waited. She had to catch him at the exact right moment or her plan would fail. Then, just as she thought she'd lost him, he stepped out from behind an elm tree and laughed as he saw her standing there holding the hogweed. But as the sunlight fell upon the soldier, Fern swung the plant into his face with all her might. He fell back in shock but when that passed, he started to laugh again - after all it was only a weed.

He unsheathed his sword and strode purposefully toward her, but Fern stood steadfast. And then it happened, the soldier screamed out in pain as red blotches appeared all over his face. Fern knew that, in the sunlight, giant hogweed causes awful blisters which burn away, angrily. The soldier now knew this too and ran back to the hunting party with tears of pain streaming down his blistered face.

Fern dropped the hogweed and scrambled through the undergrowth to find Nathaniel lying on the ground. When she appeared from the bushes he turned to face her and wiped blood from a small cut upon his forehead.

"Are you alright?" she whispered, aware of the soldier's cries in the distance.

"I'm fine," he stated, grabbing his staff and pushing himself up onto his knees. Fern ran to him and helped him to his feet and they both moved off quickly down the path to find out what had happened to Hickory.

"God damn it!" Nathaniel exclaimed suddenly, as he remembered the name of the owner of the coat of arms that he'd spotted on the banner. "A silver castle on a black background, it's Roger de Villiers'."

"Who's he?" Fern asked.

"He's the High Sheriff of Nottingham!"

"Oh no! They're coming back," the old man turned as he heard a fresh noise behind them, but it was too late.

"Nathaniel, Nathaniel!" Fern screamed as something came out of the undergrowth and grabbed her!

17: Little John

~ In Nottinghamshire the men walk tall ~

A great bear-like hand had come out from behind the bushes and tugged hold of Fern's collar. With a sudden jolt she was lifted into the air and then dropped in the clearing behind the pathway. Seconds later, as she brushed herself down, Nathaniel landed right next to her with a bump! As they looked at each other in a surprised daze, the owner of the great paw came into view.

"Oh my goodness!" Fern exclaimed, "it's a giant!" A huge shaggy-haired head brushed through the branches and smiled down at the girl and the old man. It belonged to a huge man who was at least seven feet tall and as he moved toward them his great frame blocked out the dappled sunlight.

"I'm a big lad, alright," the giant spoke softly, "though my name is Little," then he laughed and the trees all around him shook. "Still, if you are enemies of the Sheriff, you have no need to fear of Little John," he continued helping them up and then he looked surprised himself as he took in the colour of Fern's skin.

"Are you a child of the forest?" he asked.

"Perhaps," replied Nathaniel. "The truth is, we don't really know where she and her brother come from."

"My brother," Fern exclaimed, as her thoughts flashed before her, "have they taken him?"

"I'm afraid I saw them bundle something into a net. I thought it was a deer at first, but then I realised it couldn't possibly be," Little John replied.

"How can you be sure?" Nathaniel clinged to the idea that Hickory had managed to escape.

"Well, first of all, the thing they had captured was too small to be a deer and secondly it was green!"

"Oh, Hickory!" Fern cried out and she buried her face in Nathaniel's arms.

Little John bent to the ground and picked up a knapsack and a longbow. "Why are you here in Sherwood anyway?" he asked, as he swung his bow over his shoulder.

"We're looking for Robin Hood," Nathaniel answered.

"Oh, are you indeed?" Little John replied, warily.

"Yes, do you know him?" Fern asked, hopefully.

"You could say that. Look, come with me and I'll take you to him. If anyone can help your brother, then it's Robin!"

Reluctantly, they left the path behind them and followed the giant outlaw through the secret ways of the wood. For many miles they weaved their way in and out of the bushes and undergrowth and whilst they walked the light grew dimmer as the great oaks and chestnuts, hornbeams and birches grew denser and denser and the blue sky overhead was lost amongst their thickening branches.

After another hour, Little John stopped by a clump of hazel and turned to them both. "Right, from here on you have to be blindfolded, I'm afraid," and he took out two strips of linen cloth from his knapsack and moved toward Nathaniel.

"But why?" asked Fern, exasperated.

"We have to keep the camp secret and I don't yet know if you can be trusted. How do you think we have lain hidden in the forest for so many years? Secrecy is everything."

He tied the cloth around their eyes, waved his hands in front of their faces to confirm they couldn't see him and then they were off again. His gentle hand guided them, safely, along the secret path and deeper and deeper into Sherwood they went. Deeper and darker, too, as the tiny rays of light that slipped in through the edges of their blindfolds disappeared and they were soon left with only the sounds of the forest for comfort.

18: The Great Oak
~ *The heart of a forest is its oldest oak* ~

It took a long while before Little John halted. Wide and deep was the great Forest of Sherwood. One-hundred and sixty square miles of dense greenwood with a myriad of tracks and trails. A man could wander lost in there for many days and some who entered its impenetrable silence never came out again. But Little John had travelled those hidden paths for many years and where the giant outlaw now stood was the heart of the forest, in more ways than one.

"Alright, you can take off those blindfolds now," he said. Fern and Nathaniel tugged at the cloth that had taken their sight and in an instant could see again. They shielded their eyes as the sunlight drifted through the dense branches and then they blinked as the scene before them slowly unfolded. What they saw both amazed and comforted them. A whole village seemed to be living under the oak trees before them.

Ramshackle shelters of timber and leaves had been built in amongst the trees. In an open glade, a huge campfire burned brightly and lines of grey smoke drifted upward, lazily, as around the fireside, men chatted, women cooked and children played. Nathaniel surveyed the scene and then looked away and stared at Fern. He saw how she smiled as hope rose within her, but a nagging question entered his mind. If this was the home of her father why were none of these people green like her?

"Where's Robin?" Fern gripped John's arm, excitedly.

"There he is," said John, pointing over to a man sitting under the largest oak tree she had ever seen. She stared at the figure that was bent over a great longbow, fastening it with a new bowstring, and her heart missed a beat.

His back was turned as she approached and her feet made barely a whisper on the forest floor, but Robin, so alert to the noises of the woodland, still heard her approach. "A child," he said softly, without turning around. "A softer tread even than a boy . . . a girl, I think."

Fern did not hear his hushed whisperings - her mind was too intent on seeing his face. She caught sight of a dark beard with a flicker of silver. Her father had a beard - she remembered it in her dreams. Robin's green tunic and hose were similar to her own too and as he turned toward her the spring sunshine glimmered on the leaves, casting a green reflection upon the outlaw. Leaf shaped shadows danced on his face for a brief moment and for all the world he looked just like the green man carvings Nathaniel had left scattered in the trail behind them. Had that trail now come to an end? Fern's heart jumped, a pang went through her and she visibly shook before the old outlaw. But as Robin moved toward her he left the green shade of the oak tree and Fern gasped out aloud as she saw that his face was as pale as Nathaniel's and Little John's. The green pallor had been only a cruel trick of the light and the anguished girl stumbled in despair. Robin put out a hand to steady her and with a fatherly arm around her he helped her to sit upon the mossy carpet under the oak.

"It should be me that is speechless and shaking," he said, as he took in her green skin. "You gave an old man a real shock. Now, tell me who you are and why you have come to my forest?"

"We have travelled far to find you," Fern's voice quivered as she spoke. "All the way up the east coast of England, through the plague-infested city of Lincoln and to the heart of your Sherwood only to discover that you are not the man we seek."

"And who is this man you seek?"

"Our father," Fern answered, whilst

Nathaniel and Little John came over to them.

"I'm sorry, I wish you were my child. It is one of the few regrets of my life that I have no children," Robin looked down upon the girl with pity.

"It's not your fault," she replied, wiping the tears away.

"I'm sorry Fern," Nathaniel knelt down by the girl's side and held her hand in his. "It seems we have failed once again."

"Why did you believe I was your father?" Robin stood up and stared with curiosity at the green girl.

"I heard your name mentioned in a tavern," Nathaniel answered him. "The green outlaw they called you, the Lord of the Great Wood, the Master of the Forest of Sherwood."

"I see," said Robin, "and you thought I was green, as you are?"

"Yes," Fern stared up into his face. "My brother and I were found, lost in the woods, with barely a memory left between us except for the face of our father, which comes to us only in our dreams."

"And where is this brother of yours?" Robin asked.

"The Sheriff has him. He and his huntsmen caught him up by Edwinstowe," Little John interrupted.

"Well, at least I can do something about

that." He called over two of his men, spoke briefly to them and within seconds the men had collected their bows and had disappeared into the trees. "We will find out where de Villiers has taken your brother and then we'll see what we can do to get him back."

"Thank you," Fern replied, with a weak smile.

"Come now. Let's find you some food and a warm place to sleep, it may be spring but the nights are still cold," Robin said, and he and Little John led their guests towards the campfire.

ᥱ

"The older I get the more I feel the cold," Nathaniel wrapped his cloak around him and edged closer to the flickering flames as he and Robin watched the sun slip behind the trees.

"That's why I always help in lighting the fire," Robin replied. "They say a fire makes you warm four times over. First by cutting the wood, then collecting it together. A third time when you sit by it, like now, and a fourth by spreading your blankets over the warm ashes and lying on top of it whilst you sleep. Though sometimes it can get too warm. Will Scarlet got his name that way!"

"How?" Nathaniel asked, as he sipped a

flagon of ale.

"He slept on the embers one night and burnt his backside red as a strawberry. All the boys laughed and we gave him the name Scarlet instead of his real surname, which is Scathlock.

Nathaniel chuckled. "Well, he calls himself Bill Redman now."

"Very clever," Robin's thoughts drifted back to his old friend. "Tell me, Nathaniel, will he live?"

The old man looked over at the sleeping form of Fern who lay wrapped in her blanket, warm and cosy by the fireside. "What she did in Lincoln was miraculous, though it took plenty out of her. But yes, Robin, Will Scarlet will live because of her."

"Then, I owe her a debt. And Robin Hood always pays his debts, whatever the Sheriff of Nottingham has to say."

"Then, you'll help us find her brother?" Nathaniel asked anxiously.

"And tussle again with the Sheriff?" the outlaw paused for a moment and then his eyes twinkled as the first stars lit the Sherwood sky, "I wouldn't miss it for the world."

19: The Snifter, the Snoozer and the Bug-Catcher

~ Watch your purse and mind your gold, the thieves round here are very bold ~

Whilst Fern was shown around the comfortable and homely surroundings of the outlaw's camp in the heart of Sherwood, Hickory's resting place was somewhat different. It was almost midnight when he awoke to find himself lying on the hard wooden floor of a cage. Iron bars surrounded all four sides, the door was bolted and a large lock clanked as the cart that the cage sat upon bounced along the track, pulled by a ragged looking pony.

Hickory winced as he felt a sudden pain shoot up his right leg and the memory of his capture came flooding back to him. He looked down to see a blood-soaked cloth tied around his calf, but the injury stung like crazy. He pulled the makeshift bandage off and stared at the wound; the arrow had only grazed the skin but it was deep enough to be painful and more importantly it was open enough to get infected.

Hickory had nothing to tend it with other than the bloodied piece of cloth. He looked through the bars of his cage. The moonlight shone weakly through the clouds, but he had enough light to search the hedgerows next to where the cage had now stopped. He soon saw what he wanted. Upon a large clump of tall grasses a complex network of spiders' webs sparkled in the starlight. He reached his arm as far as he could through the bars and grabbed at the webs. He pulled clear a handful of the tissue-like substance and as the owner of the webs scuttled away in irritation, Hickory wound the web round and round his leg and then pulled it tight. Suddenly he had a fresh bandage. He then lay back upon the floor of his cage.

"You're a strange one!" a hoarse voice came out of the darkness.

"Who said that?" Hickory hadn't realised that his cart was one of many that were being led on by the Sheriff's men.

"I did." The little hunched figure huddled in the far corner of the cart behind Hickory's spoke the words softly, so as to not awaken the sleeping guards. "And I said, you're a strange one!"

"What do you mean?" Hickory sprang up, defensively.

"Well, I've never seen anyone make a bandage from a spider's web before, but then

I've never seen anyone with green skin before, either."

"Oh, I see," Hickory replied.

"Didn't mean to scare you lad. Just that you gave me a bit of a shock there," the man edged closer. "The name's Dobbin . . . Dobbin Finch," he continued.

"I'm Hickory."

"Pleasure to make your acquaintance, lad," the man moved forward into the moonlight. "After all, us inmates should stick together you know."

"Why are you imprisoned?" Hickory asked.

"Well, to be honest, I'm a thief . You see I used to be a snoozer and a bug-catcher but now I'm a snifter!"

Hickory looked bemused! "I don't understand."

"Let me explain," the little man was revelling in the boy's interest. "A snoozer is a fine looking fellow - best silks, fine hat and hose, who stays at the best taverns as a guest and then robs all the other guests whilst they're sleeping. Of course, no-one suspects you and you also claim to have something stolen in the morning and sometimes the innkeeper even gives you something for your loss. Unfortunately, I lost all my fine threads gambling and that was the end of my snoozing days."

"So you became a snifter?" Hickory asked, intrigued by this new criminal world.

"Oh no, I became a bug-catcher!" Dobbin shifted his position in the cart and Hickory caught sight of a long scar that cut down over his right cheek, stopping just short of his chin. "A bug-catcher lies in wait outside a tavern watching for the drunks to stumble out. Then, he knocks them over and robs them. One night though I got unlucky and the fellow that staggered out of the inn turned out to be the heir to the Manor of Edwinstowe. One of his attendants was following his young master and caught me in the act. That's how I got this!" Dobbin pointed to his foot and Hickory gasped as he saw how his left foot was unnaturally twisted at a right angle. "They hobbled me! Held me down and with a blooming great hammer they hit my ankle so hard I passed out there and then. Woke up in a ditch and dragged myself to the nearest village."

"Can you walk on it?" Hickory was horrified.

"I can get about, but it put an end to my bug-catching days so I became a snifter."

"And what is that?"

"You really are a stranger, aren't you lad!

Well, a snifter is a cutpurse; some call 'em pickpockets. Don't need to be fast on my legs, but my hands and fingers are as quick as silver," and as he spoke he slipped a small knife from his boot, stuck his arm through the bars of the cage and cut a lock of hair from Hickory's head before the boy knew what had happened. "See!"

Hickory was impressed, he remembered how swiftly Harlequin fooled the dull-witted sailors back in Orford, but this little fellow was even quicker.

"So how did you get caught?" Hickory asked.

"Clever, quick and sharp as a knife that's me, but I'm also unlucky, lad. I'd swap any of those attributes for a decent slice of luck I can tell you!"

"Why, what happened?"

"There I was in Mansfield, minding me own business, doing a spot of snifting in the market square, when I thought I'd got lucky at last. I followed behind this well-dressed gent and snifted his purse away in a blink of an eye. Full of gold coins it was, couldn't believe me luck."

"And?" Hickory was intrigued.

"Turned out to be the bleeding Sheriff himself, didn't it! I tried to put it back. I didn't want to get on the wrong side of that one. He's a real nasty piece of work. Trouble is, putting back's not as easy as taking and as I turned around to the Sheriff I dropped his purse on the floor. The coins fell out and clinked and clanked on the cobbles in front of me and before I knew it three hefty men-at-arms had grabbed me.

"What did the Sheriff do?"

"He looked me up and down with a face like thunder. 'How dare you!' he sneered, 'How dare you', he repeated, as if he was some kind of royalty. 'Throw him in a cage and take him to Nottingham,' he shouted at the guards. 'My Lord,' I pleaded, 'what're you going to do with me'?"

"What did he say?" Hickory drew closer to the pickpocket.

"He didn't say anything, lad. He just put his hand to my throat and squeezed. Then he laughed and walked away."

"Can you teach me to be a snifter?" Hickory asked, as the carts moved off again.

"I should think so lad. By the way you used that web I imagine you're pretty useful with your hands, although I have a horrible feeling my snifting days are coming to an end!"

"Dobbin, there's something I want to ask you," Hickory looked deep into the thief's eyes and the old pickpocket stared right back at his strange new acquaintance.

"What is it, lad?"

"Have you heard of Robin Hood?"

The little thief laughed, "Robin Hood, eh! Yes I've heard of 'im. Most people around here have heard of 'im. Not many that's ever seen 'im though."

"What can you tell me about him?"

"I can tell you some of the stories of his adventures, although how true they are I can't say. For a start, there's the one about how he shot a single arrow clean through three armour-clad soldiers standing in a row. Or there's the time he escaped capture during a snowstorm by fitting his horse's shoes on backwards, so when the Sheriff's men tracked him they went in the opposite direction," Dobbin chuckled.

Hickory lay back in his cage and closed his eyes and as Dobbin continued with his ballads of Robin Hood, he slowly drifted back to sleep. Not even the trundling of the carts awoke him, as the line of cages wound their way onward to some unknown fate.

20: The Saracen

~ In far away lands are deserts of sand ~

A bright, spring sunshine surfaced above the oaks of the wood and a soft dawn light shimmered red and golden rays down upon the forest floor, where Fern and Nathaniel lay asleep. All around them birds sang, squirrels leapt and rabbits ran, as the Shire Wood came to life. And then another creature appeared. He was unlike any other in Sherwood, perhaps in the whole of England, and he pushed aside the branches of the oaks and strode across the floor of the hidden camp with purpose.

He spoke quietly with a number of the men that busied themselves around the camp and whilst he undid the belt that was tied around his waist and let slip the great curved sword that he carried, he was greeted by Little John and Robin.

By the grey embers of last night's fire, Fern and Nathaniel were stirred from their slumber by the voices and as they rubbed sleep from their eyes, Robin and the newcomer crossed the glade toward them. The dark figure of the new arrival stood over them, his frame blocking out the dawn's early light, casting a

heavy shadow down upon them.

Fern threw off her blanket and then her
eyes fell upon the man and she stared up in
shock at the newcomer. Suddenly, realising

she was being rude, she dropped her eyes back to the ground. Now she knew how and why people stared at her. Who wouldn't stare when confronted by someone with skin of a completely different colour? Then she looked back up at the man in front of her whose face was as black as the night sky.

"This is Mazir Suleman Nariq Qua Mohammed," Robin smiled, as he introduced the strange warrior, "but we call him 'Teeth' because that's all we can see of him in the dark!" Robin laughed.

Fern stared at the Saracen warrior as he put his fingers to his forehead and bowed in greeting. As he did so he smiled and his grin lit up the shady glade and they saw that he was aptly named. "You see," chuckled Robin and they all broke out in laughter.

"Where do you come from?" Fern asked Teeth.

"I might well ask you the same question, my green friend," the Saracen knight replied, "but, I'm from a country far away called Africa."

"I met him whilst I was on crusade in the Holy Land," Robin interrupted, "I saved his life."

"I thought I saved yours?" Teeth retorted.

"Well, possibly," replied Robin, "but either

way we seemed to have been stuck with him ever since."

The Saracen smiled, "and I with you my friend, but I wouldn't have had it any other way."

Nathaniel looked upon the two men with wonder, "How is it that you have become companions? I thought Christians and Muslims hated each other!"

"Faith is important my friend and I still pray to the East five times a day, but tolerance of each other's beliefs is vital too and a true friendship can cross any boundaries," Teeth smiled at Robin.

"Besides, when you have seen as much death and violence upon the battlefields as we have, all of it in the name of religion, then you must look beyond the views of opposing faiths," Robin stated, thoughtfully. "All armies believe they have God on their side, but that's not possible. So, why are we fighting if we all share the same God?"

"A very good point," said Nathaniel.

"Right, now the introductions are over, tell them what you just told me." Robin sat down upon the grass as Teeth put his hand on Fern's shoulder.

"My child," he spoke softly and gently and Fern braced herself for bad news. "Whilst I was making my way back here I saw a line of horsemen travelling fast out of the southern end of the forest. There was a trail of caged carts trundling behind them."

"And?" said Fern, anxiously.

"And the cages were full of odd creatures and captured wild beasts," he hesitated, "and I'm sure I saw a green boy in one of them!"

❧

"You look so sad," Robin threw a fresh log on the campfire and sat down next to Fern. Though he had sent out more men to find out about Hickory's fate, so far none had returned and as the late afternoon sun slipped away, dusk fell and hope faded.

"I know what will cheer you up," he grinned. "I'll tell you the stories of the Wise Men of Gotham."

Fern smiled bravely but inside, dark shadows danced across her thoughts. Nathaniel, Teeth and John joined them by the glowing flames.

"I've heard of these men," Nathaniel chuckled, as he recalled the old wives' tales. "I didn't realise they were true."

"There are many things in this wide world that are more than just legends: dragons that breathe fire, devils that dance in cathedrals, intelligent Saracens, outlaws who live in the woods, even green children! So why shouldn't a handful of daft men in a Midlands village not be real," replied Robin.

"Come on then," said John, gnawing on a chicken bone, "get on with it!"

"Alright then," Robin coughed to clear his throat and then he began. "Now the village of Gotham is a sleepy little place, isolated somewhat, so the people there are a little slower than everywhere else. The most famous tale is the one of how the men of the village loved the song of a cukoo. All day and night they would happily sit and listen to the bird's delightful melody. However, as summer passed they became scared of something."

"What was it that worried them?" asked John.

"They were worried that the bird would fly away once the warm weather had gone!" Fern replied, knowledgeably.

"Correct!" said Robin. "But the wise men of Gotham had a plan."

"Which was . . . ?" John was intrigued.

"Which was to build a fence around the tree that the cuckoo had nested in and therefore keep it in the village forever!"

"Idiots!" John laughed, "it could just fly away!"

"Exactly," Robin answered, "and so their reputation for stupidity was begun."

"What else did they get up to?" asked Nathaniel.

"Well, one night when some of the men of Gotham were returning home from the inn, they saw the moon's reflection in the village pond. Of course, not being too clever, the men thought the actual moon had fallen in the water and they got worried. They sat down and planned what to do to help the moon and then spent the rest of the night trying to harness it with ropes and pull it out again!" Nathaniel chuckled and Little John fell about laughing.

"Another tale tells of how the men of the village grew angry with an eel that had been eating all their fish. So they all got together to decide what to do."

"And?" Fern pursued.

"Well, they caught the eel and then after much debate they decided on the best way to get rid of the pest."

"And what, in their infinite wisdom, was that?" Teeth inquired.

"They threw it in the river . . . to drown!" beamed Robin.

Teeth laughed out loud. "It doesn't surprise me very much. You Englishmen are not overly blessed with brains. After all, it was my people that invented mathematics, medicine, the alphabet and countless other things."

Fern giggled at the stories of the silly men and a vague memory of her father flashed through her mind as she remembered how he could always cheer her up, but before she could grasp the memory fully, a startled shout broke her train of thought.

"Robin, Robin!" the voice echoed through the trees as a hooded figure ran into the woodland camp.

"Over here," Robin rose from the fire and stood up to greet the messenger.

"News, Robin."

"About Hickory?" Fern gripped Nathaniel's arm as she ran over to the man.

"Yes," the man drew back his hood, but he turned away from the girl's anxious face and looked towards the old outlaw. "I'm sorry Robin. The boy has been taken to Nottingham!"

21: Nottingham

*~ A town of geese and a town of lace and a High
Sheriff that is a disgrace ~*

Hickory had never seen a town like
Nottingham before. Lincoln was
perhaps larger, but the wintry weather
and the ravages of the plague had left it
solemn and silent. But this place was
amazing! The streets were so crowded, the
squares so noisy and the houses so packed
together; it seemed that if you pushed one of
the crooked old timbered buildings a whole
row, perhaps even the whole town, would fall
down like dominoes. To Hickory it was like
having Wickham Market, Orford, Lincoln and
Woolpit all rolled into one. He could see the
top towers of a castle, tall church spires which
rose up above the rooftops like graceful swans
and below this, the streets bustled with carts
and livestock and people. People everywhere
- more than he had ever seen in one place!

His cage bounced up and down on the
rough cobbles and townsfolk gathered around
to stare at him. But this was not to be the
parade. The Sheriff was saving his green boy
for another purpose and he didn't want his
prize attraction being shown off to the rabble

of Nottingham. At least not until they had paid for the privilege and so a large woollen drape was thrown over the cage and suddenly Hickory's world was dark.

As the cart halted outside the castle gates Hickory quietly moved to the far side of his cage and lifted the corner of the drape. He immediately wished he hadn't. The cart had stopped upon Punishment Hill and Hickory suddenly found himself staring up at the horrifying sight of two decaying bodies. They swung from the battlements in grim unison, their heads hung limp and lifeless and from their bodies blood and entrails dripped slowly upon the cobbled ground. Hickory thought about Dobbin and glanced back at his cart, but he couldn't see him!

Underneath the hanging bodies, the terrified faces of two thieves poked out of the stocks. Hickory looked closely at the men and saw that their ears were nailed to the wooden frames to make sure they couldn't dodge out of the way of the mouldy fruit and vegetables that were being merrily thrown by a handful of youths and one particularly gleeful old hag. Hickory was transfixed and then the elderly woman went up to one of the thieves, gave him a big sloppy kiss and then started to pelt him with rotten eggs and rancid fish heads.

Next to them, some poor wretch had been caught with the Sheriff's hawk, which he hadn't returned to his Lordship in time. The punishment was to be staked out on a table whilst the bird pecked six ounces of flesh from the man's chest. The peasant in question screamed in agony as the hawk tore into his flesh and Hickory put his hands over his ears and dropped the drape in disgust. He sat back, horror-struck and pondered his own fate. What on earth was going to happen to him?

🦎

"What's he got for them, then?" The captain of the Sheriff's guard looked down from the top tower of the castle and stared inquisitively at the cages encircled in the inner bailey.

"He's got a white wolf!" replied the sergeant that stood by his side. "Very rare, apparently. From the wastes of Scotland, so I hear."

"Really? A Scottish dog! That should please the crowds," the captain spat out the words with sarcasm.

"Mind you, I've also heard a rumour that the beast's not very convincing, so its owner has helped out with a little splash of white paint," the sergeant added.

The captain laughed aloud, "Doesn't surprise me! I don't suppose the Sheriff's coughed up much money, so why provide top-notch goods."

"He could have had that Griffin from Rufford if it wasn't for that damned knight!"

"Why, what happened?" asked the captain.

"Ran it through with a lance, didn't he! Skewered it and then chopped off its head!"

"Oh, I see! Not much use then!"

"Then there was talk of some flying devil - an imp I think they called it. Seen flying over the castle last Tuesday, but nobody could catch the bloody thing. Somehow it managed to knock two soldiers into the moat, and then it pinched the Sheriff's best silk hat and dropped it in a pile of horse dung."

"Oh dear, poor Roger," smirked the captain, "so, what else has he managed to get hold of?"

"There's a bearded lady and a giant," the sergeant pointed down to the largest cage at the far side of the enclosure. "They both look real enough, although with the Sheriff you can never be certain."

"What about those three end cages. What's in there?" The captain's eyes surveyed the smaller carts behind the giant's.

"First couple are full of petty criminals; pickpockets, horse thieves and the like. Sheriff's going to hang 'em as a finale."

"How pleasant! And the last one?"

"Ah, that's his prize attraction."

"What is it?"

"A boy," replied the sergeant.

"Fantastic! Never seen one of them before," the captain turned away, bored, and looked around for his cloak.

"He's special!"

"In what way?" the captain grew interested again.

"He's green!" stated the sergeant.

"Is he ill?"

"No, he's got green skin."

"Is he painted?"

"No, he's got green skin," the sergeant repeated.

The captain slung his cloak around his shoulders to keep off the night's chill. "Interesting!" he said, thoughtfully, and as he stared at the last cage, his eyes caught sight of something else. "What's in that pit behind the boy's cage?"

"I wondered when you'd see that," answered the sergeant. He was enjoying having more knowledge than his commanding officer. "That's the Sheriff's surprise!"

"Well, what is it?" his superior demanded.

"Can't tell you sir, sworn to secrecy, I am. Helped dig the pit, see. Anyway you'll find out soon enough."

In his cage, down by the pit, Hickory slept uneasily. Something nearby was snoring loudly . . . very loudly!

"You can't leave me behind, he's my brother!" Fern looked up nervously into the face of the outlaw leader as they planned their next move.

"It'll be hard enough to make these two inconspicuous in the middle of Nottingham, let alone you," Robin stated, pointing to Little John and the black Saracen warrior. "Besides, you're in no fit state to journey and it'll be dangerous."

"He's right, Fern," Nathaniel spoke gently. "We can rescue Hickory and be back here by nightfall tomorrow."

"But . . . "

"No Fern, it's settled," Nathaniel's voice grew hard-edged and fatherly. "You wait here and prepare for his return. He may be wounded."

Fern's eyes dropped to the floor. It was true. She had felt tired and weak, she missed her brother and the worry was beginning to tell upon her health, especially so soon after her exertions back in Lincoln. "OK," she replied, "I'll stay."

"Good, that's sorted then." Robin stood up to take his customary evening stroll around his woodland hideaway. "We'd best all get some sleep. See you in the morning, and don't worry girl, we'll bring your brother back to you," he winked at Fern and then he was gone.

❧

They left for Nottingham early the next morning. Nathaniel looked upon Fern, still sound asleep under the spreading limbs of the great oak and did not wake her. He knew she'd be cross that they'd left without her, but she was sick and what could she do against the Sheriff and his soldiers anyway? No, it was better this way. He gently stroked her face and then he, Robin, John and Teeth slipped away from the encampment and took the forest trail south.

Barely moments after they had gone, Fern jumped up and grabbed the knapsack that she'd hidden under her arm and with half a dozen light steps she too left the outlaw's camp and followed the four men through the woods to find the King's Great Road and on to Nottingham.

22: The Scytale

~ Look behind the letters and learn from your betters ~

"I've got some bad news, Robin."

"You are bad news, Rat!" Robin looked down at the wizened little man who'd stepped out of the shadows in front of him. A no-good snitch that was forever spreading the gossip of Nottingham; Rat delighted in telling tales which he twisted and shaped to suit his own ends, as a potter does with his clay.

"Well, perhaps I won't tell you if you're going to be so rude."

"Fine by me," Robin made to move on but Rat couldn't help himself.

"The Templars are here," he spluttered out, hoping to annoy the old outlaw.

"Excellent!" Robin replied, hiding his concern. "Now, slip back under the stone from whence you came," and he brushed passed the little sneak with John, Teeth and Nathaniel close behind. Rat stuck his tongue out as they passed, but then Teeth turned back and glared at him and he scarpered off into the maze of backstreets!

"What are they doing here?" Robin turned to the others as they strode through the lace market and entered the narrow alleyway of Friars Lane which in turn led up to Punishment Hill and the castle.

"No idea," John replied.

"Templars! Can't stand them. Fanatics - the lot of them. Guarding pilgrims on the road to the Holy Land my backside! Money-grabbing, power-hungry religious zealots."

"You're not keen on them, then?" Nathaniel asked, drily.

"No!" Robin answered, "and nor is he!" Robin flicked his thumb toward the Saracen. "Killed his family and left him staked out to die on an anthill!"

Nathaniel's face dropped in horror as he turned to look at Teeth, but the Saracen had not heard Robin, he was too busy staring at the troop of mail clad soldiers that had just appeared outside the castle gate.

"There they are," he said, solemnly and Nathaniel, Robin and John followed the Saracen's gaze.

 ⸙

Four chain-mail clad knights stood chatting under the swinging bodies by the castle wall. Upon their white surcoats was emblazoned the red cross of the Temple of Solomon, the sign of the Templar order. Beside them, sitting on the ground, were a handful of Templar sergeants playing dice. They wore leather jerkins and iron helmets; crossbows lay on the floor beside them.

"If they spot you there'll be trouble," Robin spoke quietly, as he turned to his Saracen friend.

"Too late," John interrupted, as from behind them two more Templar Knights ambled up the alleyway.

"Un Sarrasin!" the first Templar gasped out in French staring in astonishment at Teeth. The last thing he'd expected to see in a town in the middle of England was a mortal enemy from thousands of miles away.

Robin reacted first and unsheathed the sword at his side. As he did so the Templar drew his high above his head and threw out his shield to protect his chest. The second Templar carried a lance and he thrust it forward as Teeth approached him.

Little John ran to the head of the alleyway and stood there blocking out the view from the other Templar Knights by the castle. He knew that if they were ever to rescue the green boy, then the last thing they wanted was a full-scale battle in the middle of the town square. He crossed his fingers and prayed that the clash of steel that was about to resound behind his back would not alert the knights only forty yards away.

Nathaniel didn't know what to do, whether to join in the fight or stand with Little John, so he just pushed himself up against the alleyway and watched as the mêlée began.

The first knight had seen that Robin wore no armour so he swung his blade confidently down upon him, but Robin parried the Templar's thrusting blade with his own sword and then arched his body under the Templar's shield. Before the knight could react, the wily old outlaw drew a dagger from his belt with his free hand and stabbed the Templar through the chink in his armour under his armpit. The knight had been totally outmanoeuvred; Robin seemed to dance past his defence in a singular movement. The injured knight dropped his sword and clutched at his wound and then collapsed to the cobbled ground.

The other Templar had been less sure of himself when confronted with the Saracen warrior before him. He poked and prodded his lance out toward Teeth trying to keep him at bay rather than press home an attack, but as he saw his brother knight fall to the ground he took the fight to the Saracen and that was where his strategy failed. Teeth let the knight coax him around so he had his back to the wall and then, as the Templar made a lunge at him, he stood firm. The iron tip of the lance bit into Teeth's shoulder and caught in his mail, but it meant the knight was now open to attack and Teeth knocked the Templar's hands free from the lance and with it still hanging from his shoulder, he burst forth. Raining blows down upon the unprotected knight, he knocked him to the ground with a flurry of fury. With a final stroke, the Saracen clobbered the Templar on the head and he slumped over unconscious in a heap, next to his friend.

Robin and Teeth sheathed their blades as John and Nathaniel came to meet them.

Quickly, they dragged the Templar's bodies under a cart and then turned to check on the Saracen's wound.

"I'm fine, it didn't get through my armour," Teeth said, as he drew the tip from out of his mail shirt and looked carefully at the weapon. "But this is the oddest lance I've ever seen. It seems to have something wrapped around it," the Saracen look perplexed. "What do you make of it, Robin?"

"I've seen something like this before but I can't remember where," he replied.

"I know what it is." Robin, John and Teeth turned in surprise, as Nathaniel took the spear from the Saracen. "It's a scytale!"

"It's a what?" John replied.

"A secret device used by the ancients and then adopted by the Templars. The Spartans of ancient Greece invented it and later the Roman General, Julius Caesar, used it. You threw it into your camp or to your own men if you couldn't reach them. It holds a secret message."

"How do you know all this?" Robin looked quizzically at the old man.

"Trust me, I just do."

"You have travelled far, I think," Teeth looked at Nathaniel with new respect.

"To the Holy Land and back, I have touched the walls of Jerusalem," he replied.

"So have I," said Robin. "And they were stained with blood!"

"There is something you haven't told us, though," Teeth looked deeply into the old man's eyes.

Staring back at the Saracen, Nathaniel spoke quietly and solemnly, "I know what it is because I used to be a Templar!"

The men were stunned! "One of those murdering fanatics?" Robin couldn't believe that the softly spoken old man before him could once have been a warrior for the fist of God.

"It was many years ago. A lifetime away," Nathaniel replied pensively.

"Well, what about this scytale? Is it any help to us?" John asked the old man, getting back to the business at hand.

"It depends what it says."

"How can a spear talk?" Robin was dumbfounded.

"Watch," replied Nathaniel and then very slowly he unwound a parchment strip that was bound tightly down the length of the lance.

As the old man pulled the parchment clear and laid it down on the cobbled stones, the others peered over his shoulder to look upon the inscription that now appeared before them.

"Well, that's a lot of use," Little John was not impressed. "It's a load of gibberish." And indeed the words that were inscribed upon the scytale seemed to be illegible.

```
Jo Opuujohibn dbtumf

knnj adçhmc sçd vdkk

     adaehTitJrslm
  ntkterpoeuae
```

"It's in code," Nathaniel answered him.

"Well, do you know it Templar?" Teeth seemed cross with Nathaniel.

"An ex-Templar," Nathaniel retorted, "and yes, I can work it out."

"Come on then, before the rest of them start looking for those two." Robin pointed to the bodies under the cart and gave Nathaniel a gentle nudge.

"The Templars use cryptic codes which displace the letters of the alphabet." Little John looked puzzled but Robin and Teeth were following him.

"That means in a code like this one **a** is to be read as **b** and **b** becomes **c**."

"That would make the first word on this scytale **Kp**!" Teeth was unimpressed.

"You're quick," replied Nathaniel, ignoring the jibe, "but they use more than one encryption. Try it the other way."

"You mean an **a** becomes a **z**."Robin replied.

"Precisely!"

"That would make the **J** an **I** and the **o** an **n** so the first word is **In**,"stated Teeth.

"Now, we're getting somewhere," Nathaniel looked at the letters carefully. "The first line reads **In Nottingham castle.**

"But the second line doesn't follow the pattern," even John was getting the hang of the code now. "**knnj** comes out as **jmmi**," he said, forlornly.

"So perhaps the second line conforms to the **a** becoming a **b**." Nathaniel thought out loud.

"Yes, that's it **knnj** becomes **look**," Teeth was one step ahead. "And the rest of the line reads **behind the well**."

"**In Nottingham castle, look behind the well** - perhaps this is going to be helpful after all," Robin pondered. "Maybe it's where they keep their Templar treasure!" he added, with a glint in his eye.

"Oh God! What do we do with this? My head's already aching!" John was looking dumbfounded at the last two lines of the Templar's scytale code.

```
a d a e h T i t J r s l m
n t k t e r p o e u a e
```

"I don't know!" Nathaniel replied. "This is new to me."

Teeth made a tutting noise and John turned away unable to cope with the complexity of the Templar's secret code, but Robin stared intently at the two lines of letters and after just a few brief minutes, he smiled.

"It's easy," he spoke triumphantly and then pointed to the first letter on the top line. "Watch," and he proceeded to move his finger up and down the lines from letter to letter, "**and take the Trip to Jerusalem**," he read the final part of the code out as he moved his finger along the secret script.

"So, the whole message reads - **In Nottingham castle look behind the well and take the Trip to Jerusalem.**" Nathaniel was pleased they'd cracked the Templar code, but then figures appeared at the end of the alleyway and he rolled up the scytale and stuffed it into his knapsack as more soldiers arrived.

Quickly, they strode toward the castle gateway, hoping that the Templar Knights' bodies would not yet be discovered. As a cart, laden with wine barrels, crossed the road in front of them they bowed their heads and followed it up Punishment Hill and past the cluster of Templars by the gatehouse. Hidden behind the wine merchant's wagon they slowly plodded in step with the tired looking old nag that pulled the cart along and soon they found themselves past the portcullis and standing in the inner bailey of Nottingham castle. The last place on earth Robin and his men really wanted to be!

Hurriedly, they all surveyed the busy scene before them. The Sheriff had erected a small arena in the centre of the enclosure that looked like some remnant from the days of ancient Rome and surrounding it were a succession of covered cages. In the far corner was an array of striped tents and their eyes followed the wine cart as it lumbered over towards them. Cooks, servants, pages and pie-sellers buzzed about like bees as trestle tables were unfolded, barrels of ale were unloaded and dishes of pastries were carried to and fro.

Nathaniel scanned the bailey for any signs of Hickory but was disappointed. Though in truth, he was glad he hadn't seen his young body hanging from the gibbets outside the gatehouse wall. Though there was no sign of the boy, something else had caught his eye. And he watched intently as three guards pulled at something in a large pit at the back of the bailey. Suddenly, one of the soldiers slipped and fell into the trench! A loud stamping noise rocked the enclosure and then there was a scream and the other two guards dropped their ropes and fled back to the castle keep.

Robin grabbed hold of Nathaniel's arm and led him and the others to the far wall of the castle bailey.

"Here it is!" Robin whispered and he pointed to the well.

"Well, what good is that? It's just some useless notion about a Crusade. How can we get to the Holy Land from that?" John stared despondently at the crack in the rocks behind the well. "It makes no sense!"

"It makes sense to me," said Robin, "It's a sally port."

"I'm none the wiser!" grunted John.

"A sally port is the castle's back door!" Robin replied.

"So, it's an escape route!" John had suddenly realised the tunnel's use.

"Exactly," grinned Robin. "So, when all hell breaks loose, and it will, we all meet here. Understood?"

John, Teeth and Nathaniel still looked a little bemused, but it was clear by the expression on his face that Robin knew exactly what the code meant, so they all nodded their agreement.

23: The Sheriff's Pageant

~ Keep the people glad, then tax 'em 'til they're sad ~

By midday the inner bailey was heaving with the great and good of Nottingham. A vast crowd of townsfolk mixed freely with merchants and traders, who in turn had left behind the Goose Fair in the market place and had entered the castle to watch the Sheriff's Pageant.

On the battlements, the black and silver colours of the de Villiers coat-of-arms rippled gently in the spring breeze and as a troop of trumpeters blew their horns, the Sherrif and his entourage appeared from the doorway of the castle keep. Waving to the crowd, Roger de Villiers and his cronies made their way down to the arena, signalling the start of the festivities.

They took their places in their seats and whilst wine was poured for them the trumpets and drums sounded again and the Sheriff's Pageant began. "What a clever idea this was, your Lordship," one of de Villiers' minions ingratiated himself with the Sheriff.

"Yes, my liege, a truly excellent idea!" smirked another.

"I know, Piers. A cheap bit of entertainment,

some gratuitous violence and the odd hanging and this lot are well pleased." The Sheriff looked scornfully down upon the people of Nottingham and sipped at his wine.

It was a good idea though, the Sheriff thought to himself. He knew the townsfolk were fickle. Keep them fed and entertained and they would cough up his taxes, not to mention his trade tariffs, road tolls and protection levies. He was slowly amassing a small fortune and as long as he could keep it hidden from the King and from that damned outlaw, then in a couple more years he could retire in real splendour to his estates in Yorkshire.

A loud trumpet drew the Sheriff from his scheming thoughts and as he wiped wine from his greying moustache and settled his ageing frame into the hard wooden seat, the first of his entertainers entered the arena.

Nestled in amongst the rabble standing around the ring, with their faces hidden by their hoods, four members of the crowd watched the proceedings with special interest.

"Still no sign of the boy?" Robin whispered the words to Nathaniel and the old man shook his head.

"Nothing." he murmured, in reply.

"Well, we just keep watching then. I've a

funny feeling that we'll be seeing him soon enough if I know the Sheriff." Robin's eyes darted around the arena, but it wasn't a green boy that entered first but a man dressed in purple robes breathing fire.

"How on earth does he do that? Look there's no burning at all!" Little John stared in awe as bright red flames ran swiftly along the fire-breather's arms.

"He spreads the sap of the marsh mallow plant over his skin, it provides a protective layer which allows him to endure the heat," Nathaniel answered.

"How do you know that?"

"The girl told me," he replied, referring to Fern. "She has a way with plants and flowers."

Had Nathaniel looked behind him at that moment he would have seen the very same green friend slipping through the crowd and quietly making her way up the steps to the castle battlements.

As she moved, however, an old hag grabbed Fern's wrist firmly and turned her hand over. "Tell your future, young woman?" she cackled, but then she recoiled as she stared down at a green palm. Fern hurriedly pulled her hand free and was gone before the old crone could say anything! She sped along the wall-walk of the battlement, slipped behind an outcrop of stone and cast her eyes back down upon the arena, the Pageant and the expectant crowd.

It had been an uneasy journey to the town for Fern. She had followed the tracks of Robin and the others easily enough through the forest, but travelling along the King's Great Road had been hard going and it was only the determination to save her brother that had got her this far. Now, looking down from her vantage point, her quick eyes had already spotted the faces of Nathaniel and Teeth in the crowd and she knew that Robin and John would not be far away. But there was no sign of Hickory and she had no idea what Robin's or her own next move would be!

As the fire-breathers, jugglers, acrobats and dancers left the arena to a ripple of applause a new arrival entered and started to address the crowd. At first Fern thought she recognised the fellow, for he had a long cloak of bright quarters and the red and green shades danced about as the strange man jigged to the centre of the ring. But it wasn't her friend, Harlequin, who'd helped her back at Orford Castle, for this entertainer's eyes were much more sinister and he wore a wicked grin upon his painted face.

"People of Nottingham gather around,
see the parade of the creatures we've found."

He sang the words out to the crowd as
behind him a strange array of attractions
entered the showground.

"Here's Huffle the giant who is so tall . . .
he even makes the castle look small.
Now here my lads is something to be feared:
a cackling old woman with a beard!
Look out, look out, here's a wolf of white,
snarling and growling and ready for a fight.
And last of all, safe inside his cage . . .
we've got a green boy in a terrible rage!"

"Oh God," muttered Nathaniel, as he saw
the face of his young friend peer out, terrified,
from behind the iron bars of his pen.

"We'll never be able to free him if he stays
in that cage. Look at the lock," Robin
mumbled, as Hickory's cart was pulled
forward into full view.

"So join in the fun and don't be sad,
our dear old Sheriff's not all bad!"

Back in the arena the ringmaster bowed
and turned to clap the Sheriff, who smiled
down reluctantly at the crowd.

"I wish I had my damned longbow," Robin
snarled.

"Why?" asked Nathaniel.

"For with an arrow I do swear,
I'd aim to part that riddler's hair!"

Nathaniel smiled at the outlaw's own rhyme and then he felt something hit the end of his nose. He looked upward and realised what was happening and then he heard the shouts of derision. "You might not need that longbow, Robin. Looks like he's about to get his comeuppance anyway. It's starting to rain!"

Across the arena, a pool of white paint was appearing under the cage of the white wolf as droplets of rain washed away the animal's fake colour. Nearby, the crowd had watched in annoyance as the white wolf turned rapidly into a mucky brown mongrel and then their cries of anger echoed right across the enclosure as all eyes turned to the beast's cart.

Large puddles formed quickly in the middle of the ring and suddenly the giant lost his footing and fell! He tumbled clumsily and then another gasp of displeasure rang out, as the giant seemed to crumple in two. In fact, what was quickly apparent was that this had been no giant at all but two men; one sat upon the other's shoulders. A well-fitted cloak had covered them very cleverly and they'd rounded off the deceit with straw padding.

To make matters much worse, the top half

of the giant had fallen towards the bearded lady and in a vain effort to stop himself tumbling, he fell against her and grabbed her beard. The elaborate 'beard' of horse-hair was pulled clean off her chin and now lay limp in a puddle looking like a drowned rat! The now 'un-bearded lady' shrieked with pain and a good measure of embarrassment and ran crying to the castle keep.

Chaos ensued; the crowd jeered, rotten fruit was thrown and all eyes quickly turned upon the riddling ringmaster and the angry Sheriff. Thinking on his feet, the ringmaster looked up at de Villiers and drew a finger across his throat. The Sheriff nodded in reply and suddenly three men in chains were brought forth into the arena by a line of guards. The ringmaster danced over to them merrily and as he led them to the waiting gallows, the crowd grew quiet again.

Upon the scaffold, two black-hooded executioners checked their ropes whilst the condemned men plodded towards them, eyes downcast, unable to face the sight of the gibbet before them. From his cage Hickory watched the sad scene, suddenly flinching at the sight of the figure at the back of the line. It was his friend the snifter, Dobbin Finch!

Gleefully, the ringmaster kicked the first

criminal up the stairs and then he pulled the next one by his ears. The crowd laughed, cruelly, and then the hooded executioners pushed the two convicts onto the scaffold and slipped nooses over their heads.

Somewhere behind Hickory a drum beat solemnly and the crowd around the arena held their breath. The executioners kicked away the stools from under the condemned men's feet and they dropped with a terrible jolt! Necks stretched, heels dangled in mid air and as they gasped vainly for life, Hickory turned away as one, then the other, stopped their jiggling and the arena cheered.

Turning back, Hickory now saw that Dobbin was being led up the scaffold steps whilst the two dead men were cut down. The ringmaster was having fun with the bodies; pretending to talk to them and raising their arms to wave to the crowd. But then his eyes fell upon the limping form of Dobbin Finch.

He immediately dropped the corpses' arms and danced his way over to the hobbling pickpocket. He kicked away the stick that Dobbin used to help him walk and the little thief fell down the stairs bumping his head on each step. The rabble around the ring laughed, but as Dobbin arose a red trickle of blood oozed from a nasty gash on his forehead and Hickory's anger rose.

One of the executioners, obviously bored with the proceedings, strode down the steps, picked Dobbin up and slung him over his shoulder. The other executioner prepared a new noose and Dobbin was stood upon a stool ready to be despatched. The drum sounded again and the snifter's balding head was slipped through the rope. Then the ringmaster, relishing being the centre of attention, ran onto the scaffold and kicked the stool from under Dobbin's feet. However, he did so before the executioner had tied the hanging rope securely around the crossbeam of the gallows and the pickpocket fell to the floor and landed on top of the ringmaster.

"Another disaster," the Sheriff muttered under his breath, as around him the crowd grew impatient again. He signalled for the ringmaster to come to him and while Dobbin was tied up for another attempt later, the Sheriff knew it was time for his main attraction to be unleashed if he was to save the day and keep the townsfolk happy.

"Yes, my Lord. What would you have me do?" The ringmaster had retreated to the Sheriff's side.

"We'll have to use it now," de Villiers whispered.

"But my Lord, it's too dangerous!"

"I don't care!" His anger rose. "Now, get back out there you fool!" and he pushed the ringmaster out to the baying crowd.

The ringmaster regained his composure, wiping sweat from his forehead and then grinned as he addressed the mob once more.

"Wait, wait dear folk of Nottingham town,
Do not cry and do not frown.
Our dear Sheriff has one last beast,
To bring to you upon this feast."

An uneasy, yet expectant hush settled around the arena as a line of soldiers pulled and pushed something dark and large toward the entrance of the ring. Suddenly, a huge beast appeared. The whole crowd gasped in wonder at the strange creature that now lumbered across the floor of the arena and the Sheriff looked down with a satisfied grin upon his face. The ringmaster looked around to check the beast had arrived and then he introduced the Sheriff's star attraction to the people of Nottingham.

"From distant lands this killer was found
and now he's here upon this ground,
With coat of steel and a sharpened horn,
here's the fearsome Runnicorn!

Hurriedly, he crossed the ring to Hickory's cage and from his belt he took out a great long iron key. He unbolted the door of the cage, pulled Hickory out and handed the confused boy a wooden shield and a small dagger. At the ringmaster's signal, the guards let go of the ropes holding the huge beast and as he backed nervously out of the ring, he gave Hickory a vicious push toward the monster at the other end of the arena. Then as he followed the guards out of the ring and closed the wooden door behind him he shouted out,

"And now everyone for your delight,
the Green Boy and the Runnicorn will fight!"

24: The Runnicorn

~ From far-away lands is a beast of wonder, with feet that pound like raging thunder ~

Hickory couldn't believe his eyes. The runnicorn was enormous; twice the size of a cow and almost as tall as a horse. It must have measured nine feet long and from top to toe it appeared to be encased in solid grey armour, just like some huge overgrown knight.

The creature's head was stranger still; a hulking lump of grey that hunched forward out of its powerful, armoured shoulders, with two giant horns sticking out of its forehead. Hickory stared in wonder at the animal and it stared right back through him with black, soulless eyes.

Suddenly, the beast flared its nostrils and stamped its feet and Hickory realised it was far too late to try talking with it. Instead, he gripped hard upon his shield and braced himself for impact as the runnicorn charged toward him.

The collision was terrible! Splinters from Hickory's shield spun off in all directions and the crowd around the combatants screamed out loud as shards of wood thumped into

them. Once the panic of the onlookers had died down, all eyes returned to the arena, where the dust from the runnicorn's charge had begun to settle.

The crowd scanned the ring for signs of life, though they expected to find Hickory a crumpled heap of green on the ground before them. But somehow the beast had only caught Hickory's shield and the boy had dived out of the path of the onrushing beast at the last split second. Now, sword in hand, he picked himself up from the ground at the far side of the arena and as he did so the crowd actually cheered. From his vantage point above the throng, the Sheriff looked down and scowled.

But Hickory was far from safe; the runnicorn had turned its massive frame round and had already begun to stamp its feet in readiness for another attack.

"What in God's name is that?" Robin stared past the guard and blinked as he gaped at the runnicorn.

"I have no idea," Nathaniel replied, dumbfounded.

"Me neither," answered Little John.

"I know what it is," Teeth stepped into the crowd and stood behind them. "I have seen one many years ago, far to the south of my country, deep down upon the wide grasslands."

"Well," Robin asked, "what is it?"

"The tribesmen down there called it a *rhinos*," Teeth whispered the name under his breath, as if it was an evil word. "It's very dangerous!"

"I'd worked that out for myself," Robin retorted. "How do we stop it crushing the boy?"

But before Robin received an answer Teeth had already slipped through the cheering crowd and stood at the front of the arena where he cupped his hands and made a strange grunting noise.

Immediately the *rhinos* stopped in its tracks and stuck its huge head upward and started to sniff the air around it. Teeth continued to make the odd sound and the beast grew more and more agitated. It had forgotten all about Hickory, who quickly ran to the side of the arena, as all eyes concentrated on the *rhinos*. Then, in a sudden explosion of frustration, the creature started to bash the arena wall. Whatever it was searching for, its inability to find it was driving it crazy.

Teeth had attracted the animal for long enough and with one last effort he repeated the strange sound and ran. The ground inside the arena shook as the *rhinos* stamped its feet in exasperation and then it ran straight at the wall next to where Hickory lay hidden. The boy managed to dive out of the way again just in time as the *rhinos* narrowly missed him and crashed through the wooden fencing. The watching crowd screamed as the wall splintered asunder and the *rhinos* broke free.

Wooden shards from the fence flew through the castle bailey like spears and one of them thumped into the leg of the ringmaster, who had tried in vain to grab hold of Hickory. The boy had fled but the ringmaster had been knocked to the ground and as he tried to stand, his long quartered cloak got caught up in a tent peg. Unable to move he screamed for help as the *rhinos* charged toward him, but nobody heard his cry and the last thing he saw was a great grey shadow above him and then he was trampled into the ground!

"What on earth did you do?" Robin asked the Saracen as he ran back to him.

"Let's just say I distracted the beast."

"But how? And what on earth was that strange noise you were making?"

Teeth laughed, "It was the mating call of a female *rhinos*. The tribesmen of the bush use it to trap the creatures in their pens."

"Very clever!" Robin replied, but then he looked behind him as a heavy pounding sounded out aloud. "Problem is," he shouted, as the thudding noise grew louder, "it's now following us!"

Teeth looked back to the arena and sure enough the *rhinos* was charging right toward them.

"Well, I'm not waiting around to watch you wed a *rhinos*," and with that Robin pushed Teeth toward the well and they both ran for their lives.

As it pursued them, knocking down everything and everybody in its path, the Sheriff's archers and the Templar sergeants ran swiftly along the battlements of the castle, and with a sharp call of command from their captain, they halted and drew back their bows. Two dozen arrows sped down into the square like silver sparks from a blacksmith's hammer. Half of them bounced harmlessly upon the cobbled ground, several more thumped into the wall of the arena and three rebounded off the hard grey armour of the *rhinos*. But two arrows had been more carefully aimed and struck the beast on the back of its hind legs. Hamstrung, the mighty runnicorn came crashing to the floor in a cloud of dust and rolled over with a heavy thud!

From her vantage point on the battlements, Fern had watched the events below her unfold, with a mixture of horror and relief. She had felt fear, rage and utter helplessness when Hickory was in the arena, but she grinned with joy when she saw him escape with Nathaniel and run toward the back of the bailey. Now she had to do something fast. With the *rhinos* down, some element of order was returning to the chaos within the castle grounds, but yet another line of Templar sergeants was now clattering along the wall walk toward her.

Spying one of the Sheriff's prized peacocks, she moved next to the bird which obligingly fanned its tail. Fern hid behind it as the Templars passed her by. But then she gasped with fear as the men loaded their crossbow bolts and aimed them down at the fleeing figures of Robin, Teeth, John, Nathaniel and Hickory. What could she do? There were at least six soldiers and there was nothing to help her on the battlements but a pile of broken shields and a couple of wicker hives. But hives meant bees, she thought for a moment . . . perfect!

She tip-toed along to the first hive and shook it wildly, whispering soft words into it, and within seconds a swarm of bees appeared and headed straight for the Templar crossbowmen. The insects buzzed around the men and flew inside their chain-mail and then they started to sting. The soldiers dropped their crossbows, cursing, and those that could fire found their bolts flying off in all directions and missing their intended targets down by the well.

Quickly, Fern sprinted past the twitching Templars and taking the steps down from the castle wall two at a time, she reached the floor and then sped across the bailey.

"What the hell are you doing here?" Nathaniel was angry, but relieved.

"Saving your skin," Fern replied, breathlessly, as she hugged her brother.

"Come on then," shouted Robin. "Let's get out of here!" But, as he spoke, a stray bolt bit into his shoulder spinning him around.

"Damn!" he muttered, as he broke off the flight and threw it to the ground.

"Robin, are you alright?" John held his old friend steady.

"Just a graze," he stated and then as the Sheriff's guards spotted them he led them down the dark tunnel that was cut into the rock behind the well and they all took 'the Trip to Jerusalem'.

25: Kirklees Priory

~ It's not the bite of a snake that causes death, but the venom it spreads with its evil breath ~

They entered the tunnel blindly, stumbling around like new-born puppies and with nothing to light their way they thumped against the rock walls, knocking chunks of crumbling sandstone to the floor. But Robin seemed to have no fear and he led them onward, around sharp corners, through narrow passages and downward, ever downward.

At one point they all stopped to catch their breath but heard faint clashes of steel behind them, so they quickly moved off again. Then, at last, they saw a thin shaft of pale light ahead of them and suddenly they had escaped the cloying, breathless air of the secret tunnel and they spilled out into the daylight like tiny fish coughed up from the belly of some great whale.

They shielded their eyes from the sudden sunlight, which streamed down upon them through the gaps in the poorly thatched roof above. Once they had regained their vision they saw that they were stood in a large yard surrounded on three sides by lines of beer barrels. On the fourth side was the timbered wall of a building and on it was painted a white shield with a red cross upon it.

"Where are we?" John asked, brushing a cobweb out of his hair and staring in concern at the shield design.

"Is this a Templar stronghold?" Teeth asked in a whisper.

"No," replied Robin, assuredly. "This is the Trip to Jerusalem!"

"What do you mean?" John spluttered.

"The Trip to Jerusalem is the name of the inn." Robin pointed to the building and smiled. "The Templar message on the scytale was to say that the castle's back door led through a secret tunnel in the rocks to this tavern. You see the word 'Trip' doesn't mean journey, it means somewhere to stop; crusaders to the Holy Land would gather here before making their voyage. I should know - this is where I started from."

"So what are we waiting for? Let's have a beer," John grinned.

"No time for that, I'm afraid," Nathaniel was looking backward at the entrance to the secret tunnel, "we're still being followed."

He was right, loud voices reverberated down through the passageway and a glint of steel shone out from the darkness. "Quick," shouted Robin, "help me block the entrance."

Hurriedly, all six of them pushed, pulled

and kicked at the lines of barrels in the brewer's yard and with one final shove the casks of ale came crashing down just in time, as the first faces of the Sheriff's guards appeared before them.

"That was close!" Teeth grinned. "Now, show me your wound Robin," Teeth held Robin's arm tightly.

"What wound?" Robin replied, innocently.

"I saw the bolt strike you," Teeth answered and held his friend in an iron-like grip.

"Oh, it's nothing." Robin smiled but as he did so, blood fell to the cobbled floor of the yard and he stumbled.

Little John held him up as Teeth drew back Robin's cloak and found the shaft that lay buried in the outlaw's shoulder.

"I thought as much," the Saracen looked worried.

"Let me see?" Fern took one look at Robin's wound and her eyes fell. "It is deep, but with some herbs and a place to rest it will heal."

"Well, we can't risk going back to Sherwood," Robin laid back against the barrels and closed his eyes in thought. "The roads will be infested with de Villiers' men."

"Then let's make for Kirklees Priory. The nuns have always been our friends and they will help all of us to recover," John stared at

Robin with concern and saw how the green boy looked almost done for.

"Good idea," Robin pushed himself up again. "Kirklees it is. Now let's just see if those Templars have left their horses nearby. I'm sure they wouldn't mind if we just borrowed a few. If I remember rightly, the castle stables are right next to the inn. Come on," he laughed, with a fading twinkle in his eye.

❦

Whilst a scarlet sun fell silently to earth and disappeared beyond the western horizon, a wide arc of geese banked in silhouette and flew gracefully across the dying sky. Far below them, a loud thudding echoed across the neatly farmed fields surrounding the ancient Priory and its many outbuildings, as the sisters of Kirklees closed their shutters to the outside world and the coming night. And when the darkness came, candles were lit in the refectory, the dormitory, the infirmary and even in the little bedchamber high up in the Priory gatehouse.

"I can't do anything. There's something here I don't understand." Fern's voice was quick and anxious as she paced around the tiny room.

"That's because it's poison," stated Nathaniel, matter-of-factly.

"Another Templar pleasantry?" Teeth was angry.

"Yes, I'm afraid so," Nathaniel held the shaft that had been stuck in Robin's shoulder and studied the tip carefully. "Look here, there's a stain of black." They all peered in to see the tiny patch of colour on the point of the shaft. "The Templar crossbowmen dip their bolts in a deadly mixture of hemlock and monkshood."

"I can't believe that people use the powers of the plants for evil!" Fern stared in horror at the crossbow bolt, as tears trickled down her face.

Nathaniel looked down upon Robin, "There's no antidote, I'm afraid."

"How long have I got?" Robin spoke calmly.

Nathaniel looked to the floor, "Not long."

"What about one of your leech doctors?" asked Hickory.

"Too late for that I'm afraid, lad." Nathaniel put a hand upon the boy's shoulder as all of them fell silent around the outlaw's bed.

"This is all our fault," Fern's eyes were red from crying. "You wouldn't be lying here if it wasn't for us."

"No, my child," Robin raised his hand to quell her tears. "It's not your doing. I am old and my time is coming to an end." The old outlaw hesitated for a moment, his eyes took on a faraway look and then he spoke softly and eagerly. "But there is something you can do for me."

"Gladly," replied Fern, "what is it?"

"It is not an easy task, but there is someone I would like to see before I die."

"Who? Who is it?" Fern exclaimed.

"Marian," smiled Robin. "My Marian!"

26: The Maid

~ Time heals all things ~

The road to Southwell Minster was choking with travellers. There were wagons piled high with vegetables from the rich farmlands around the Wash, carts carrying lace from Nottingham, drays rolling along with beer barrels from Burton, drovers driving cattle, shepherds herding sheep and swineherds pushing pigs to market. A line of white robed Cistercian Monks, heading to the great cathedral of Peterborough, passed by a troop of black robed Dominican Friars, heading in the opposite direction to York. A company of Royal soldiers marched in good order toward Newark Castle, a band of brightly dressed troubadours danced their way to the Horse Fair at Hallaton and a grey, ragged band of flagellants rang bells and whipped their own backs as they strode, sombrely, away from the ravages of the plague in Lincoln. And in between all this, a great mass of pilgrims buzzed about like insects, as they headed in great swarms to the Minster at Southwell.

Weaving in and out of the slow-moving traffic on the Great North Road, Fern and

Nathaniel rode as fast as they could upon the Sheriff's stolen horses. They had left Hickory behind to rest his wounds and to keep Robin company while they endeavoured to fulfil the dying outlaw's final wish.

"You mean they all want to see someone's finger?" Fern asked the old man, in bewilderment, as they approached Southwell.

"Not just anyone's finger, but St. Paulinius' finger," Nathaniel replied, explaining the pilgrims' progress toward the Minster. "It was he who brought Christianity to this area, in Saxon times, by baptising the locals in the River Trent."

Fern looked at Nathaniel in utter disbelief, but as expected, when they finally arrived at the Minster it was packed to the rafters with pilgrims. They were everywhere; kneeling down in front of the altar, staring at the beautiful stained glass window of King Edwin and praying by the reliquary box which held within it the index finger of the blessed Paulinius.

They dismounted from their steeds and tied them up near the cloisters. There were the usual stares of wonder as Fern pulled down her hood, but either the pilgrims thought they were seeing a miracle or they were just too rapt in prayer to notice. Either way she was not approached and they both quickly made their way through the Minster to find help.

The first person they found was an old nun in a black surplice, who was bent crooked tending to some herbs by the cloister entrance. Nathaniel asked if Sister Marian was to be found nearby and without raising her head from her precious patch of rosemary and thyme, the aged nun pointed in the direction of the infirmary and moments later the two of them entered the hospital chamber.

Inside was a row of beds where men, women and even children lay in varying states of distress. Some had broken limbs, some suffered from fever, some were on the mend, while others were fading fast. As the groans and cries of the sick echoed through the infirmary, three or four nuns dashed from one bed to another dispensing medicine and sympathy in equal doses. Instantly, it brought back bitter memories to Nathaniel and Fern, but fortunately the *Foul Death* had not touched Southwell and this was just the everyday trials of life.

Then, one of the nuns looked up from her duties and spied the two strangers at the end of the corridor. Her kindly eyes fell upon them as she wiped the brow of the young lad she was tending to, whispered some words of encouragement in his ear, rose and made her way toward them.

"Are you ill?" the nun looked at Fern with concern.

"No, no," answered Nathaniel. "That's her natural colour!"

"Oh, I see. Well, how can I help you then? "

"We are looking for someone," Fern replied.

"Who?"

"Her name is Sister Marian," said Nathaniel.

"And why do you seek Sister Marian?" the nun spoke cautiously.

"Someone sent us to find her and take her back to him," Fern stared at the nun, thoughtfully.

"Oh really!" the nun exclaimed. "And who on earth might make such demands upon a nun other than God himself?" she demanded.

"This person is a very old friend," Nathaniel was surprised at the nun's outburst.

"I see," the sister replied, "so what's so urgent that this old friend requires to see her now and who is he anyway?"

"His name is Robin Hood and I'm afraid he's dying!" Fern spoke in a hushed voice, remembering that Robin's name was the name of a wanted outlaw.

The nun's face dropped in dismay and she lost all her colour. She turned away from the two strangers and looked back at her charges in the beds of the infirmary. She called over to one of the sisters and spoke in whispers to her and then she turned back to Fern and Nathaniel. "Well, I'll need to collect a few things before we go."

Nathaniel and Fern looked at each other in surprise. "You mean . . ." but the nun interrupted before Nathaniel could finish.

"Yes," she stated softly," I'm Sister Marian!"

27: The Longbow

~ It's the wood of the yew that makes the longbow shoot true ~

"I'm sorry I didn't turn out to be the person you thought I was," Robin was sat up in his bed sipping a bowl of warm pottage, whilst Hickory stared out of the window of the Priory gatehouse.

"It's not your fault," the boy replied from across the room. "Perhaps we will never find our father," he said, as he returned his sad gaze to the woods far below.

"Don't say that lad, I'm sure you will. Fathers and sons should be together."

Hickory's eyes fell upon Little John and Teeth who were practising with their longbows in the fields below and then he turned to stare at Robin's great bow that sat in the corner of the room. "Try it lad," Robin had noticed Hickory's interest in the weapon. "Go on!"

Hickory rose from the bench he was perched upon and crossed over to the warbow. He picked it up slowly and admired the workmanship that had fashioned it.

"Have a go," Robin grinned through the pain that coursed his veins. Hickory held out the giant weapon and pulled back the drawstring. "Wow," he said, unable to pull the cord back very far at all.

"Amazing isn't it? You need to develop strength and practise daily to become a truly great archer." Robin smiled at the boy's attempt. "I've seen arrows penetrate through chain-mail, even plate mail, if you hit the target straight on. I've seen arrows pass through one man to hit another behind. I've even seen them fly through tree trunks. Such is the power you can find from the longbow."

"What type of wood is it made from?" Hickory asked, as he stroked the bow.

"It's yew." Robin replied. "It's made from one perfect piece; there are no knots or blemishes and through patience and experience I tapered it to fit my body perfectly."

"How does it bend so well?" Hickory handed the bow to Robin.

"It has the softer sapwood on the back and the heartwood on the belly of it."

"And what about the bowstring?"

"It's made of flax linen and then covered in beeswax to waterproof it." Robin found an arrow lying by the bed and held it up. "As for the arrows, they can be made from any wood, but the heads are solid chunks of iron with these barbs on them to make them more painful to pull out."

"I see," Hickory studied the arrow carefully.

"And the feathers?"

"They are fledged with goose feathers. They're the best and some fletchers say that the left side of the goose is where to get the finest."

"How long have you had the bow?" Hickory asked.

"First time I used it was at the Siege of Messina, when the English archers drove the Sicilians from the walls. Richard the Lionhearted preferred the crossbowmen, but it was the longbow that broke the siege. A good archer can fire off a dozen shafts in a minute you know. Your crossbowmen can only manage two in the same time; all that cranking and placing the bolt in the groove takes far too long. Most of them are dead before they can fire at the enemy." Robin closed his eyes and recalled that day many years before. "The sky was full of arrows: 20,000 of them falling like black rain. Inside Messina, they said that for a full hour no man could look out of doors without having an arrow in his eye."

"Perhaps I will see such a thing one day."

Hickory closed his eyes too and imagined the faraway battles.

"Hope you don't, lad. I remember when we entered the city gates and the scene of destruction left there. The trebuchets and catapults had done their damage to the tall towers and the high walls, but it was the arrows that had killed and injured the men. Those alive stumbled about with shafts in their legs, arms, chests and worse of all, their faces, like gruesome hedgehogs. Full of spikes some of them!"

Hickory put the bow down and returned to watch Teeth and John use theirs. Behind him, Robin closed his eyes and fell back to sleep. Then, as Hickory scanned the green cornfields beyond the Priory boundaries, his eyes were drawn to the copse of trees on the horizon. He felt something stir inside him and he saw a small figure limp through the trees. Pushing his face closer to the open window he watched the stranger like a hawk and then, as the spring sunshine fell upon his face, Hickory recoiled in surprise. "It can't be," he muttered, "it can't be him . . . surely he's dead!"

The man who stood in front of Robin and the others looked grubby and half-starved. "So, tell me why you're here?" Robin asked him.

"I've come to warn you that Guy of Gisbourne has been despatched," Dobbin Finch replied, as he munched hungrily on a crust of bread.

"I see," said Robin, pushing himself up against his pillow. "And why would you do that?" he asked with suspicion.

"Because if it hadn't have been for you, I'd have been hanged by now!"

"Dobbin's a snifter," Hickory spoke up in defence of his friend. "The Sheriff was going to execute him."

"Oh yes, I remember you now," Robin paused. "How do you know about Gisbourne though?"

"I managed to escape when that runnicorn went wild and I hid under the Sheriff's carriage. When he turned up next to it I listened from underneath and I heard him scream, 'Find Gisbourne and tell him to get me that damned Wolf's Head'!"

"I see," said Robin.

"Talk was about that you were ill and had been brought here," Dobbin continued, after sipping some ale. "So, I thought that seeing as you'd done me a favour, so to speak, I should return one to you."

"Very good of you, Dobbin," Robin smiled.

"I don't understand!" Hickory looked bemused. "Who is this Guy of Gisbourne?"

"He's a 'geldman'," John answered.

"What's that?" the boy was none the wiser.

"It means he's an assassin," Robin stated, coldly. "He's a paid killer; a bounty hunter who's been sent to kill me. He's tried before but then we've always been hidden away in Sherwood and he's never found us."

"But here we're much more exposed!" Teeth spoke solemnly and crossed to the window and stared outside.

"I'm glad to see that my dead body is still worth a lot of money," Robin joked. "Although why Gisbourne doesn't just wait a few days, I don't know!" Robin laughed out loud, but nobody else joined him.

❦

Toward sunset, a cluster of horsemen rode up to the copse on the outskirts of the Priory's fields and quickly dismounted. They tied their horses up to a dead elm tree, unsheathed their swords from their scabbards and in single file, as the sun began to fall, they disappeared into the undergrowth.

Up in the gatehouse Hickory stared through the half-light, his nimble eyes watching closely as Teeth and Little John followed the men through the trees like long shadows. Then, he gasped as he saw the Saracen warrior raise his curved scimitar and fall upon the men. Distant shouts and screams echoed on the breeze. John's quarterstaff whirled and crashed like a tornado and moments later four of the men lay face down in the dirt.

But one man had escaped the ambush and that man was Guy of Gisbourne. He gripped hard upon the pommel of his sword, drew back his chain-mail coif and sprinted toward the tower where Robin lay asleep.

Hickory saw him coming and ran to the great longbow, grabbed a handful of arrows and tried to draw it again, but once more it was too much for him. As the boy began to panic he felt a presence behind him and then firm hands took the great bow from him.

"He's mine," the voice behind stated grimly and turning around, Hickory was amazed to find Robin standing over him. He moved away from the window and watched in wonder as Robin placed the arrow and drew back the bow in one effortless movement. Then, peering down into the darkening priory courtyard, the old outlaw found his aim and let fly his shaft

Hickory ran back to the window just as the

arrow sped downward. It caught Gisbourne with such power that it burst through his chain-mail shirt, splitting the metal asunder and carried on straight through into his heart. He was dead before his body hit the ground!

Minutes later Teeth and Little John appeared and they dropped to their knees to check the bounty hunter was indeed deceased, and then they cast their eyes upward to the gatehouse window.

Hickory saw their glances and then turned back to find Robin struggling to stand. The old outlaw fell back into bed, exhausted. "I hope they return with Marian soon," he half-whispered as Hickory helped him back under the bedclothes. "I can't last much longer!"

28: Brother Robert

~ *Faces echo down through time* ~

It took a while for Sister Marian to collect what she needed for the journey, so whilst she saw the Abbess and gathered her belongings, Nathaniel and Fern entered the West door of the Minster and strolled down the nave. They passed by the beautifully carved pews, the altar and the Pilgrim's Chapel and were both entranced by the elaborate stonework and the wonderful designs that surrounded them.

"This place is as beautiful as the cathedral at Lincoln," Fern stared at the eagle shaped lectern by the pulpit. "But one thing still confuses me."

"What is it?" asked Nathaniel.

"Your stone houses are so tall and so magnificent but many of your people live in poverty and have little food to eat. How is it you can justify these great buildings?"

Nathaniel stopped and turned to her, "You are right, of course. Sometimes it takes an outsider to see things clearly, but many believe that constructing a great building like this is how we bring Heaven to mankind and mankind to Heaven." Nathaniel spoke deep in contemplation, as much to himself as to Fern.

"Come on," he shook himself from his thoughts. "There is one place in particular we should see." He tugged at the girl's arm, led her past a line of Benedictine monks and found the entrance to the Chapter House.

"Oh, Nathaniel, how wonderful!" she cried, as the old man opened the door upon walls covered with smiling faces.

"I thought you'd like it," Nathaniel grinned.

In front of them, in fact on all four walls around them, was a forest of stone leaves. And poking out between the sculptured ivy, the delicately shaped nettles and the carved bryony, were dozens of green men.

"Who carved all this?" Fern's voice quivered.

"I have asked around," Nathaniel answered, "but sadly no-one seems to know. Yet it may at least mean that someone, somewhere, has seen your people."

Fern sat down upon a pew and shut her eyes in thought and Nathaniel closed the door behind him and left her there, encircled by the green men, in quiet reflection and with hope renewed.

❧

By mid-afternoon Marian appeared from her

cell and greeted Nathaniel and Fern by the herb garden.

"Are you ready to leave?" asked Nathaniel, seeing her approach.

"Very nearly," she replied, "but there is someone I wish to take with me."

"Of course, a companion. A fellow nun." Nathaniel understood that one of the sisterhood couldn't leave the confines of the nunnery without a travelling companion; it would be quite improper!

"No," replied Marian, to the old man's surprise, "it's a boy, actually. He is a novice here."

"I see," said Nathaniel, looking a little bemused.

"It will do him good to see . . ." Marian stumbled on her words. "It will do him good to see the outside world," she finished.

So, she led them along the cloisters to the dormitories at the far end of the Minster and as they turned a corner, Marian smiled as a young monk closed the wooden door of his tiny cell and turned to meet them. He was tall and slender, like a young tree, and his eyes twinkled brightly as he saw them. Almost immediately, both Nathaniel and Fern recognised something familiar about the young man but neither of them could quite put a finger on what it was.

"This is Brother Robert," Marian introduced the novice and he bowed his head in recognition, then he took Marian's travelling bag for her.

"Well, we had best be getting on," Marian was keen to reach Kirklees before it was too late.

"Yes, speed is of the essence, I fear." And with that, Nathaniel led them all to the stables and by late afternoon they were riding with all haste toward the Priory and the dying outlaw.

29: The Last Arrow

~ When an arrow falls from the sky, someone good is sure to die ~

"**O**h Robin!" Marian's eyes fell upon the grey-faced figure lying in the bed.

"Thank God you're here, girl," the old outlaw smiled. "I didn't want to die holding hands with either of these two," he grinned through the poison induced pain that coursed his body and pointed at Teeth and Little John.

Marian ran to the bedside, knelt down upon the wooden floor, gripped Robin's hands and buried her face in the bedclothes.

"Don't weep, my love," Robin whispered, as he loosened a hand and lifted up her chin. He wiped away her tears and kissed her forehead. "Why did we leave it so long?" he murmured. "Still, you're here now." Marian smiled and then Robin noticed the figure standing close behind her. "And who's this?" he asked. "Not a rival for my affections, I hope!"

"Well, I suppose he is really," Marian rose from the bed and ushered the novice monk forward. "This is Robert." The young man nodded his head. "He's . . ." Marian stumbled and then braced herself, "he's your son, Robin!"

The old outlaw's face looked first shocked, then bemused and finally pleased. "Come forward," he raised himself up and embraced the young man. "A dying man's final wish," he muttered weakly, as Marian too embraced him.

Whether Robin had ever known about Robert wasn't clear and how much Marian had told him wasn't known by any of the others standing quietly in that room. What was clear was the joy in the outlaw's eyes as Teeth, John, Nathaniel, Fern and Hickory all silently backed out of the room to leave Robin and Marian and their son alone to talk.

❧

An hour later, Marian lit a candle in the bedchamber and opened the door and called the others back in. She smiled, weakly, as they approached, "It's nearly time," she said softly, before John wrapped his huge arms around her. Quietly, they all gathered around the outlaw's bed.

"One last arrow," Robin's voice quivered. "This is the silver arrow that I won nearly thirty years ago at the Sheriff's archery competition. Do you remember, John?"

"Aye, Robin, I remember alright."

"Help me old friend," Robin pushed himself upward and then Little John lifted him out of bed. Teeth handed him his bow and Robert opened the shutters by the window.

Then, a slight figure burst through the chamber door and Dobbin Finch puffed and panted before them.

"Robin!" he gasped.

"Yes, what is it, Dobbin?"

"The Sheriff's dead, Robin!"

"How did it happen?" asked John.

"It seems that his own bodyguards had had enough of the bitter old devil, so they tied him to his carriage and pushed it off a cliff. All of Nottingham is rejoicing!" Dobbin grinned.

"And so it ends," Robin muttered, as his thoughts drifted back in time to his many encounters with his old adversary. "Though I will see him again very soon. Come on, John."

Braced against his old friend, Robin stood by the open window and held up his beloved bow for the last time. "Lay me down where this arrow lands," he whispered through the pain. Then he pulled back the bowstring and let fly.

It was as good a shot as ever he'd made. As good as the silver arrow competition, as good as when he faced the Sicilians at Messina or even when he'd killed a Saracen warlord on the walls of Jerusalem. Hickory and Fern ran to the window, amazed to see the shaft fly so far. It sailed out of the opening and far across the fields to land softly in the sun-strewn grass of the late afternoon. It was a shot no other man could have made. It was a shot from a character in an ancient myth or a half-forgotten legend. It was a shot only Robin Hood could have made!

They watched the arrow fall like a tumbling sparrow hawk and they smiled to see it land on the far horizon. But then a soft crying behind them made them turn their faces back to the bed. Sweet tears slipped down Marian's face as she held the old outlaw's hands in her own and then buried her head in the woollen blanket that covered him. Robert looked downward and put an arm around his mother's shoulders as Little John bent his huge frame and gently closed the outlaw's eyes. Robin Hood was dead.

Silently, they came to bury him. From near and far, by horse, by cart and by foot. And as late afternoon approached, three days after he had died, a large gathering had appeared in the fields behind the Priory, to pay their last respects to Robin Hood.

The children were there, as was Nathaniel, Marian and Robert. And they watched in wonder as the empty green fields around them suddenly became crammed with people. Towns and villages now lay quiet and still, shops had been shut, markets closed, pilgrimages abandoned and farmsteads left idle for the day.

Down at the Priory entrance, Little John and Teeth met each new arrival and it seemed as though they knew them all and each one had a memory to share with them about Robin. But at last, as the final individuals made their way down to the graveside, Little John closed the Priory gate.

"Wait for me!" a thin, frail-looking figure called through the dusk and John laughed when he saw him. He wrapped his great arms around the latecomer and then ushered him over toward the children.

"Will Scarlet!" Hickory exclaimed, as he recognised the man.

"Yes indeed, children! Here by the grace of God and Fern's tender care."

Fern smiled and shook hands with him. "I'm glad to see you again."

"Well, I'm only sorry I didn't have time to help you properly, back in Lincoln," Will said, sadly. "I could have saved you a journey and plenty of heartbreak too, I believe."

"That's true, but then we never would have

met Robin and that was worth all the hardships we went through," Hickory answered.

"Very true," Will looked toward the grave. "And he was always worth meeting. And here's another of our infamous band," Scarlet grinned at the minstrel who crossed over to them.

"This, children, is Allan a Dale. A singer of ballads - many, of course, about Robin and the rest of us."

"Well, how interesting," the minstrel smiled as he saw Fern and Hickory. "I've heard of you. Although I must confess, when the fellow I met told me about you, I didn't believe him. Not a very trustworthy chap, you see. However, he was right about you. In fact he said he was a good friend of yours!"

"Who is he?" the children asked in unison.

"He said he has many names, but you would know him as Harlequin."

The children grinned. "Oh, yes, we won't forget him!" they replied together.

"He told me that you are searching for your father."

"That's right," answered Fern. "We thought it was Robin, but sadly it was not."

"And before that we thought it was the Wild Man of Orford," Hickory took up the tale.

"And so you continue your quest?" Allan asked.

"We have no other choice," Nathaniel replied, despondently. "But where we go from here, I don't know."

"Perhaps I can help," the minstrel's eyes sparkled as a thought came to him.

"How so?" Nathaniel looked curious.

"There is a story; a legend of a warrior. I do not know his name," Allan replied, "but I do know that in the tale he is called the Green Knight."

"And where does he live?" the old man was intrigued.

"Far away in the land of Cornwall, on the western tip of England."

"I see," Nathaniel smiled at the children.

"Allan, it's time," Little John called across the gathering, whilst the sun slipped toward the horizon behind his great frame. The minstrel left them to think as he took his lute and joined the band of outlaws. Grey they were now, old and solemn, with deep lines etched across their faces and silver hair upon their heads. Yet there was still an inner fire within them, for they had lived and fought with Robin Hood and that would not be forgotten.

They stood over the grave in silence, heads bowed. They were all there: Allan a Dale, Will Scarlet, Much the Miller, Tam Farthing, Jack Ramsholt, the priest they called Old Tuck and of course, Teeth and Little John. It was they that carried Robin's body to the open grave and they that gently laid him down into the dark earth.

Then, those that had known him well filed by; his band of woodland followers, his outlaws, his trusted friends. And then Fern passed by the grave and dropped in a daisy. Its white petals fluttering in the breeze like a tiny bird. "For hope," she whispered, and then turned away. Hickory followed her and laid the mighty longbow next to him and Nathaniel let fall a sheath of arrows. Next came Robert and he held Robin's sword. It was a beautiful thing, forged in Jerusalem, and it shone like a ray of sunshine as he laid it down upon his father's chest.

Last of all came Marian. She held her head up high and smiled. The sadness within her would never leave her now, but she carried with her memories of Robin that would last her through her remaining years. And of course she had Robert to remind her always of the old rogue. She knelt by the grave and spoke so softly that no one around the grave heard what she said. Then she laid down a tattered piece of cloth. Many in the crowd around were surprised to see her offer up something so old and ragged-looking, but of course they didn't know that she'd carried it around with her for almost twenty years, or that it had travelled all the way to the Holy Land and back, or that it was the hood from whence their hero had gotten his name!

Finally, relinquishing her hold upon the hood, she rose and that was the signal Allan a Dale was waiting for. Whilst Teeth and Little John took up shovels and covered their friend's grave with soil, the minstrel played gently upon his lute and sang these words:

The Last Lament of Robin Hood

It was in the woods of Sherwood
where Robin made his name.
A proud and noble leader
a man they could not tame.

The Normans called him Outlaw
the dreaded Wolf's Head.
But there is no doubt, without him
we would all be dead.

His prowess with the longbow
gave him fame throughout the land.
Yet he was also cunning
in the way he led his band.
Robin did defeat the Sheriff,
the barons and the church.
He was the Saxon rebel
who knocked the mighty from their perch.

He stole from the greedy rich
and gave to the needy poor.
He will be dearly missed
that brave green Outlaw.

As the words drifted away into the coming dusk, a solemn line of carters, smiths, weavers, fletchers, thatchers, millers, serfs, servants and bondsmen, silently passed by the grave. For many hours the people - his people, filed along in due reverence, for their hero was gone. Then, they weaved their way back down to the Great North Road and silently they wandered back to their humble homes.

And so, whilst the sun went down, Nathaniel and the children drew up the reins of their horses and turned away from the great Forest of Sherwood. But Hickory glanced back and looked on in wonder. For young Robert had pulled on his own hood. And as he stood against the sunset his silhouette seemed to grow. He spied Hickory watching him and gave him a wink that was full of his father's confidence and in that instance Hickory knew that the legend of Robin Hood would live on.

Then, as darkness descended, Hickory turned back to his sister and the old man and together they rode west. West, to the war-torn lands of Cornwall and the ancient realm of the legendary Green Knight.

. . . To be concluded.

Historical Note

Robin Hood is the most famous and popular folk hero in Britain and I believe that his legend is based upon lots of different men that rebelled against authority during the medieval period.

Bishop Hugh was a real figure and was Bishop of Lincoln from 1168-1200. After his death he was made a Saint.

Other legends touched upon in the novel, such as the Lincoln Imp and the Wise Men of Gotham, are enduring folk tales that should not be forgotten.

As for the Green Men Carvings mentioned in the story, well, once again they really do exist and if you look carefully enough in and around the churches referred to on the maps then you can see them for yourself.

Glossary

Bishop	-	*High Church official*
Cathedral	-	*Large Christian building*
Dean	-	*Head of Cathedral Chapter*
Egypsies	-	*Medieval term for Gypsies*
Gibbet	-	*Post for hanging criminals*
Gildmaster	-	*Head of a Gild of Craftsmen*
Jerkin	-	*Sleeveless leather coat*
Mail	-	*Flexible armour made from iron rings*
Palisade	-	*Wooden fence or wall*
Quarantine	-	*Isolation to prevent the spreading of infection*
Saracen	-	*Arabian follower of Islam*
Templar	-	*Soldier of military order of the Knights of the Temple of Solomon*
Tisane	-	*Type of herbal tea*
Vial	-	*Small bottle for medicine*
Zealot	-	*Fanatic*